THE WARRIORS CYCLE

THE SWORD OF ANATH

Marilyn A. Hudson

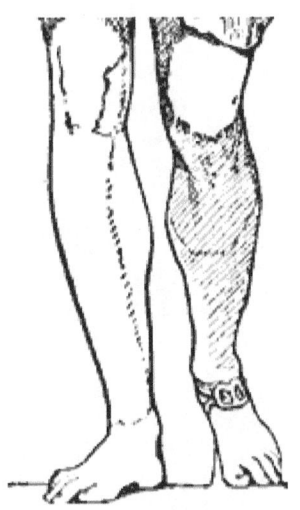

Whorl Books

WHORL BOOKS

Hudson, Marilyn A.
The Sword of Anath. The Warriors/
Description: In an ancient time, a primeval malevolence leeches out setting in motion a clash of good and evil. One woman holds the ability to keep the evil at bay – can she accept the challenge? Can she fulfill her destiny?

Subjects: 1. Fantasy fiction.   2. Anath (Fictional Character). i. The Sword of Anath.   ii. The Warriors Cycle: The Sword of Anath.

ISBN-13: 978-0692373903 (Whorl Books)
ISBN-10: 069237390X
PZ 7 H88

Note: historic notes in preface material are works of fiction.

"The song of the raven's rise...
over the field of mourning.
Shields beat in time to fearful hearts...
The skies are sulfur, all our tears are blood.
The Walker is no more and the warden sleeps.
Who stays the evil, who will dream the way?

The halls of meeting are silent...the beast attacks the door.
fearsome thing awaits...

All is dust, all is decay and the song of the raven grows
strong...where shall we run in our desolation?
Where shall we hide in our destruction?"

--Fragment of the <u>Song of Enlil</u>
Translated from cuneiform tablets dated at between 2334–2154 B.C.
By Dr. Karen Houston

The Song of Anath

I am she who walks between the worlds.
Doomed to wonder corridors long and stark
Forever locked within... never seeing home
Down the eternal corridors of shadows
I forever roam.

I stand in place to guard the ways;
With heart of fire and sword of stone... I fight
Keeping the growling, hunting beast in this place
Locked in [this] darkness... keeping it from the suns...
I see all the ways....future and past are bright...

It was my choice to stay and serve.
Shouting, I lifted my sword arm high...strong
To swear the sacred oath
My sacrifice was for that other world;
The place of wind's sweet kiss
Beneath a wine dark moon [or sky].

"I am she who walks between the worlds!"
Down long and spiraling trails
"Stand tall, find strength" I call...
Down the undying corridors of shadows
I forever wander. "Others may forget [fail to remember?]...
Remember [be here in this time?]...
I am the one... Anath!"
---Translation of stele found in 1820 by Francois Dupon
Additional translation by Dr. Karen Houston.

Chapter 1

The insatiable twisting flames feasted on the burning buildings and then spat deadly glowing sparks high into the night sky. Noise seemed to erupt from everywhere. A harsh clash of metal mixing with the shrill screams told her the battle still raged in pockets all around her. Heart pounding, she stumbled into the remains of one building, and hid in the shadows trying to grasp what was happening. The sudden assault had caught them all off guard and death could claim them all before dawn. Gritting her jaw she concentrated on the events of just moments before.

The simple feast of her people to celebrate the end of the hard work of the harvest had been like all the others. Joyous dancing, bountiful food, new wine and enjoyment of a season completed were eagerly anticipated by everyone.

She had enjoyed the cooling breezes as the sun began to set and she made her way to the bonfire. The children, laughing and calling taunts, had chased each other through the town square. Bright eyed young men had hovered around giggling young women wearing their finest clothes and jewels. Old men hefted large goblets of wine while they sampled the roasting meat or the crusty fresh breads. Musicians played merry tunes and people laughingly danced and sang. Hard work behind them they were ready for a pleasant evening and most made fun of those who danced with too much wine and too little skill.

Then *they* arrived. They swooped out of the dark shadows of the night with swords flashing bright in the firelight. Suddenly, there was blood soaking into the sands, and laughter died as bodies fell to the sand. Panic was a living thing as her people ran from the attackers.

Stunned, she could only stare at first and then she sprinted forward to pick up a sword dropped by one of the villagers. Old, and not as sharp as needed, it was enough as she raced to beat back the vile shadows in human form. Minutes were like hours and the marauders seemed invincible as she threw herself into the battle. Everywhere were the screams of horses and the shouts of men. In the distance, backlit by the flames from a burning building she saw her sister and some of the others leading the children away.

Something cut into her flesh for her distraction and she felt a hot flash of pain. She turned her back on the fleeing people and went on fighting the strangers. Tall, dark of beard and heart, she recognized the ebony leather they wore. *Mot's men.*

Well-rehearsed marauders whose every breath was drawn to kill would find little to halt them in a weary and unpractised farmers. Even the few warriors they had, although capable and brave, would be hard pressed to survive this assault.

Finally, all she and the few others left could do, was to run and hide. As they hurried away the pounding of her heart and the thud of their footfalls could not erase the sounds. Those echoing screams would be with her till her dying day.

Now, after evading the men and seeing the others break off heading a dozen different ways, she paused against a wall. Every muscle screeched and there was a dreadful burning with her every breath. Despite the wad of cloth she had tied to her waist, she could feel the warm blood flowing out of the wound in her side. When she cautiously touched the wound, biting her lip to hold in the cry, her fingers came back painted a dark and glistening red. Too much red...

They are determined to kill us all. Why? *Our village has nothing of value.* Simple farmers and craftsmen were the only inhabitants. *I cannot understand such wanton killing; I will never understand it.*

At a sound behind her she awkwardly stumbled further into the shadows between two buildings. Falling against the wall, she closed her eyes willing herself to focus and to think.

In mere minutes, two of the mercenaries rushed past. Swords drawn, they searched for her people; they never saw her in the shadowed entry to the alley. They rushed past and she was alone once more. For a brief moment they had been illuminated by the fires raging. They were strangers to here but she had seen such men before. Death was their only prize. Destruction their only spoil.

It took all of her effort to stand erect as she pushed away from the wall of rough stone and crept up the narrow, hidden passageway. The wound in her side was an agony with each step. It still bled heavily; she had to get it tended to or risk dying.

Wiping the moisture on her skirt, she looked around and tried to think. She wanted nothing so much as to simply lie down and give into the pain. Maybe in that oblivion the images in her head would leave her. Tears coursed down her face but she ignored them because more important than her grief and pain, was the real threat to her own life.

As a child a dog had gone mad, frothing at the mouth and attacking everything. She remembered how it had stood in the yard and swayed looking like the familiar animal but also so different. Her father and another man had faced it with swords, hesitantly, but when it bounded towards them their swords had met in the chest of the dog. *It was mad*, her father had told her, *and would have killed you without mercy or even awareness of what it did.*

The menacing shapes prowling through the streets would also kill without awareness. They were aware of what they did, however, and seemed to enjoy their work.

I should have killed him that first day. When they were first reported, she thought as she gritted her teeth. Gasping, she sprinted toward one of the buildings. *So much would have been spared, and so many lives would still live, if only things had been different; if she had been different.*

"Mot, you will pay. I swear this now." Behind her the tongues of flame continued to feast on all that she had known and loved since a small child. "I don't know how you will pay for this madness...but you will be made to feel the pain you've brought my people tonight."

First, though, she had live.

Turning toward the east, she scrambled down the rock-strewn hillside and only then paused to look back. Spilling out from the town were silent shadows of her people hurrying to escape and find sanctuary somewhere safe.

The elders had taught them if trouble arose, seek out the far hills, and so they did so now. Leaving behind their charred lives.

The ache in her side was like a troublesome companion as she trudged across the grazing lands. Her goal was the purple hills spread across the distant horizon.

Life had once been so very different...

Chapter 2

The sky was a bowl of white-hot flame as Hasai and the old donkey staggered to an exhausted stop. The spindly trees and dead leaves provided only the most meager shade in the pitiful oasis. Dry scrub plants withered in the sun.

Hasai squinted into the milky sky before he slid from the animals back. "Such a miserable tree is a poor shade but it is enough to rest for a while."

Pulling the water bag off the animal's back, he slapped the rear of the creature. "Go on! Go find what you can to refresh your old bones, my friend."

He watched briefly as the animal wondered over to the brown and meager mud pool that passed for water and then turned to crawl under an emaciated tree for its pathetic shade. Even the wind was cruel today. Like a wanton child, it tossed fistfuls of sand as it raced past, instead of leaving any refreshing coolness.

He wanted nothing so much as to be home with his wife and his children. He was getting too old to follow the trading roads across these forsaken lands.

In the distance, a sliver of mountain range lay like a temptation far across the sands. Their colors reminded him of plums and grapes. So cool and refreshing they looked in the distance. A stark contrast to the view closer to him. Sands that stretched for miles and all around was the white fire of heat dancing like rollers on far silver waves.

Eyes squinting he surveyed the landscape. *The sands shimmered like the waters. That was so long ago*, he thought wiping away the sweat from his face. The more he looked the more clearly the memories of those undulating waves of the seas. He had once seen such things from the deck of a Sea people trading ship when he was a child.

"So cool and so far away," he murmured taking a drink from his water bag. "To be young again, especially on a day like this."

He dwelled, for long contented moments, in a happy memory of miles of cold water and lovely exotic women. *Ah, to be a youth once more,* he thought, *with the world to explore and new women to win.*

He had thought he would be one of the priests back then. He had the visions and the dreams. Strange sights had filled his head and many came true. Then…why had they stopped? *Did the prophecies I had really ever stop*, he wondered drowsily, *or did I simply stop paying attention to them*?

A hot gust of wind slapped him suddenly, driving more of the hot coarse sand into his face, disturbing his reverie. "It is much hotter today and too windy. How can a man rest?" Sitting up he began wiping the sand from his face. The grains of sand whirled around him as if they could not decide which direction to travel.

Spirals of sand gathered and like fingers danced across the hot plain going this way and that before fading as a cool breeze seemed to settle down around him. He shivered in the sudden cold.

As he looked out at the still shimmering sands, he paused suddenly, at something he glimpsed on the western horizon. He wiped his eyes and squinted again into the distance. He had to be seeing things. Through that shimmering wall of heat it looked like a woman walked towards him.

A young woman, tall and lean, a sword buckled at her waist, and her long brown hair held back by a bronzed headband. She seemed unaffected by the heat or the wind as long legs confidently treaded across the golden sands. Indeed, the air, now she was closer, seemed strangely cool and unlike the previous heat of the day.

The metal of her accoutrements reflected the bright sun. Tiny spots of light danced over his face and body from them. She sauntered up to him, her gait agile and assured, as if striding across a shimmering golden sea. Boldly and unafraid she walked right to where he sat on the sand.

"Greetings, old father, would you share a drop of water with a traveler?" She spoke slowly as if uncertain if he would understand. The voice was low and soft. There was an inflection to her speech that was compelling with an undertone of authority.

Old Father; an ancient greeting that, and very formal, yet her way was causal and easy. When she spoke, she had an accent but he could not place its source in his mind. It seemed faintly familiar, but his mind could not call up a memory of where he had ever heard one similar. Maybe it was something he heard when a child or as he traveled with the sea people?

She smiled at him then and he looked into eyes like deep waters, cool and mysterious. Without a word, dumbstruck like a beardless youth faced with the village beauty, he handed her the water bag. Was he dreaming in the heat of the day?

No, she was real and she stood before him with eyes like burning sapphires. The air around them seemed different as if the moment was fecund with significance. He felt something stirring to life in his soul.

A strange sensation came over him. Not for years had he had a vision. The prophecies of his youth had dwindled to the faint and too easily forgotten dreams of an old man. Now, however, words bubbled from his lips like fresh water from a powerful hidden spring. *"She who walks between the worlds...."*

As the old man paused in his story, little Anath wiggled closer to old Hasai, gently reminding him of her presence. The old man sat under the leafy green vines shading the resting place and the child sat on the bench leaning in the crook of the frail arms. The setting sun bathed everything in a soft amber light. A cool breath brushed past bringing needed respite from the day's heat.

"Then the camel reared up and the old thief toppled off into the pile of hot steaming dung. That was where the young prince finally caught him and retrieved the jewels."

"What of the princess?" demanded the child turning bright but demanding eyes towards him.

"She was found trapped in a tiny jar. They summoned all the magicians and together. They broke the spell and freed her to rule her land once more."

The little girl clapped her small hands and laughed with delight, "Good!" She snuggled closer to the frail man. He did not mind. Her warmth felt good on such a cool night. They brought back memories of his own family so many years before.

His old bones felt the change in temperature too much these days. Each creak called up old times, old pains, and things that might have been. To be young, he thought with a sigh, it is wasted on children.

"Tell the other story again Hasai! Please, I love the story of how you met my Mother."

Hasai smiled at the girl, and as she settled down to listen, he saw himself reflected in her wide sapphire eyes. She looked so much like that noble woman. Her younger sister, Asherah, asleep on her pallet in her room, was shorter but had the strong dark eyes of her father instead of the blue of her Mother.

"Again?" He sighed as she nodded. "I had been returning from trading with the far tribes. I had silks, jewels and fine wines. The weather had been so dry and the wide plain was nothing but a dry empty land without shade or water."

He closed his eyes to recite the tale carved into his very bones over the years from his many retellings of the moment.

"Your mother, Astarte, she came out of the sands that day, lost from her hunting party and not bothered by the fierce heat of the day. She had carried with her a fine and strange sword and had the look of one used to giving orders. She was a special person, a very gracious and strong woman who took in a tired old man to live out his last days in the mountains, surrounded by family and friends. She was a blessing herself…"

Zeni found them slumbering as the twilight shadows deepened into inky pools. Hasai was snoring lightly, his chin on his chest, on the garden bench in the cool evening air with the master's child in his arms. Zeni had more than a few gray hairs in her own head but the old man seemed ancient.

She remembered him coming to the village, so many years ago, when she was new married. Many years later, her master Dagon had invited him to this house when he grew too old to go trading. His wisdom, and his visions, had been valued for many years to Dagon and many others.

"Silly old man, "she muttered fondly reaching out to pick up the child. "Master Dagon will have my hide for letting Anath be out in the chill. She must be well when he brings home his new wife."

"Here, let me take her," said a voice behind her.

She turned to see the Master's oldest son, Hadad, standing there. Son of the master's first wife, Hadad was now almost as tall as she was, but still sometimes had the manners and kindness of a small youth. He was standing at the crossroads. Soon he would be a muscular and tall man. Then, like so many others, he would think of little but hunting, women and wine.

"Thank you Hadad. Put her down to sleep quietly. Do not wake little Asherah." She told him as she rose. She winced as she heard old bones crack loudly in the night. "I will see to the other old one here."

"She loves the stories of her Mother," Hadad muttered hefting the girl into his arms. She was lightweight but long limbed. She would no doubt look him in the eye when she was fully-grown. "Silly little girl."

Zeni smiled to herself and said nothing. Hadad liked to pretend he cared nothing for the small sisters who had come into his life when he was five. They adored him anyway.

He pretended male indifference. Zeni knew better, so Zeni smiled. As the sounds of Hadad's sandals faded away, she helped him to stand, and led him away to the servant's quarters.

"He wages a battle within himself," Hasai said of the departing youth. "There is pain in him still at the loss of his mother. Sharp and unhealed."

"What boy would not mourn such a loss?"

"He blames his father too much. For marrying again, for fathering other children, and most of all for living when his mother died. Such blame breeds bitterness. It is a wound he will not allow to heal. It will fester in him and cause trouble one day."

"Come, let's get you to your bed."

The moon, full and bright, was rising over the mountain peaks and the scent of the crimson flowers on the wall brought memories of other nights long ago. They paused in the small courtyard.

"The child so loves the story of how I met her Mother," Hasai noted in a frail voice. It was clear which child he meant. He always meant Anath. He leaned his head back to stare into the heavens above them and at the stars glittering everywhere.

"Yes, she does." Zeni settled down beside him and they sat lost in their own thoughts for many minutes. Theirs was a companionable silence. It was borne of many years working together in the same household and loving the same children.

"That little one; she is very like her Mother."

The old man is very talkative this evening, Zena thought. Usually he shuffled sleepily into the bedroom and fell into a deep sleep, unaware others had urged him to his bed. He had been very ill over the last winter and she saw he was weaker now than he had been.

"I think her little sister will be much like her as well." Zeni added to keep him awake enough to move him toward his cot. "She copies all her older sister does now."

"I remember that day so well in the desert. She was like a goddess walking across the magic waters instead of dry, dusty sand."   "Yes, Hasai, you have often told this story." She murmured. "It is a wonderful story. You're a poet. But you must go to bed now."

"When I saw her, I could have called her '*she who walks on the sea*' because that was what it looked like that day in the heat. A tall figure she came through the dancing heat currents. It caught my breath."

"Yes, old man, yes, you have told me this story many times."

"Instead of the greeting I had intended, I spoke a prophecy. I opened my mouth but the words were not mine." He seemed to be staring off into a far off place only he could see.

The wind had stilled and the lights seemed strangely bright in the dark silk of the sky. "It had no meaning then and none now. I have so often wrestled with those words but the sense of it slips through my fingers." His voice was nearly a whisper. "*She who walks between the worlds.*"

"Yes," Zeni said soothingly. Her back was beginning to ache and she longed for some sleep before the dawn came again. "You have told it well and often old friend. It is time for bed now."

A ripple traveled across the courtyard then, as if the earth and the sky moved. It shuddered through them and their very bones rattled. Zeni gasped as she looked around. Frantically, she clutched at the wall and looked around in fright trying to see if great cracks split the courtyard. *Why isn't everyone awake and fleeing the walls of the house*? She glanced at the old man. *What magic is this old one?*

Instead of staring at the earth that shuddered beneath their feet, the old man stopped, straightened suddenly, and stared up at the sky. His face looked as if decades had fallen from his shoulders.

Zeni shivered in the sudden strangeness of the moment.

"Here sit down, old one!" The earth shook again but this time it was so different. As if something beneath them grew restless and was shaking off its slumber the ground rippled. Strange spears of light ripped the dark sky; lightening without a storm. Were there evil spirits aboard to steal their souls?

Beside here, suddenly the man spoke but his voice was strong and odd. It was as if another spoke through him. He paced around in swift energy appearing more youthful as he moved. It was as if he was casting off the decades that had bent him over. His eyes glowed with an uncanny radiance.

"It is all so clear to me now! The things I can see. There is so much…"

On his face there was a sheen of joy and his skin glowed in the dark.

As they had so many years before, words bubbled from his lips once more like the fresh cold water from a hidden spring. "*Now* I understand. The little one; it is she who will walk between the worlds!"

"Anath?"

"Yes, it is so…but her path will be filled with danger and struggle."

"She is only a baby!"

"She is the one. There is a choice she must make. She will walk a path no one else can tread." His face took on such a look of terror she feared he would drop dead at her feet. "Oh, but there is much she must suffer." He slumped heavily against her then and she staggered under the frail weight. "She will need to be strong to endure and fulfil her destiny. Pray she decides the way carefully!"

He seemed different now, as she hurried him along to his cot, the last moments of energy and vigor now forgotten. He seemed somehow more drained and empty. There was a lightness to him as if he were an old bag of dried husks.

Fearfully, dreading what she knew must be coming, she struggled to get him to his cot.

Beneath her feet, the earth – shifted – and the night grew icy. Chill fingers of bitter cold danced across her flesh. A wall of frozen cold, solid enough to touch, closed around her and she cried out.

Hurriedly she lifted one of the stick like arms over shoulder and led him through the door back into his room. He made no sound as she brought him to his bed.

He stumbled onto the pallet and there lay as one already dead. A touch of her fingers to his throat felt the feeble, far too faint, beating of his heart. She took one of his gnarled hands in her own. It was all she could do for now.

Tears in her eyes, she kissed his hand. "Sleep, old friend, sleep."

As another blast of the sudden cold wind wove its way through the dark night a night bird called anxiously across the night. Its plaintive call went unanswered and the stillness hung heavy with fear.

Zeni felt the heartbeat grow stronger and she rose to go to her own bed. Sleep was always the best cure for troubles. The sudden loss of the moonlight hurried her to the doorway. In the sky grasping and twisting murky fingers of clouds suddenly obscured the moon. Again she felt the cold and pulled her cloak closer. Something walked the darkness tonight and she did not understand what it was.

Zeni frowned, glancing back at the bed where the old man now slept, then finally stepped back into the courtyard and hurried to her room. She only breathed as the bolt went down on her door. The last few moments had been so out of the ordinary she needed the feel of the warmth and light in her own quarters.

In the shadows, her fingers found the niche where her house god token was stored. She whispered prayers there in the dark. They were the prayers she had learned as a girl. She felt no better, though, as she pulled her blanket over her tired body. How could the earth move but no one awaken? How could the night grow so cold and foul like that? And Hasai, how had he looked so young? The night had turned so strange and she feared such mysteries boded nothing but ill.

Her last thought was of little Anath, the old man's strange prophecies, and the strange events following his words. A saying from her childhood rose in memory, *the future is a dark night,* and shivering anew, she offered prayers for all of them.

If only the child's mother had lived.

Chapter 3

"No! Don't hold it like that Anath!" Turga hoisted the bow to his own shoulder. Although his hair was the color of the ash from the fire his arm easily pulled the arrow back. Squinting, with his one good eye, he focused on the mark, and then he pulled back, "Watch now."

He released the arrow and, with a thud, it hit the target dead center.

"Make the action smooth and sure."

He watched the little girl glance nervously to where her father stood frowning in the distance. He appeared to be watching all the children and youth as they trained. He did not look toward any particular child and certainly not to the spot where Anath worked.

Turga, though, saw where her thoughts were going. He squatted down by the girl. He held the bow out to her. "Here, pretend I am showing you something very interesting about the bow."

Brilliant blue eyes flashed up to his weathered face but seeing his small smile, she relaxed. *There is spirit in the child,* Turga thought.

"You show great promise little one. One day I think I would hesitate to face you in battle."

"My father…"

"Is a powerful man who expects much from his children," Turga sighed. "There are many types of fathers. Some men encourage competition for attention from their offspring. They say it is to cause them to learn to fight. I think it is more so they will just feel powerful and in control. A better father cares equally for all his children. He may expect much but he also gives much in terms of protection, provision, and, if one is lucky, expectations."

"So you are saying that despite his being distant with me, he does care for me." Anath sighed as she spoke. "I just want to please him…but it seems like I never do."

"You – Anath – you must want to master the tools of the hunt. You are nervous and fearful because you are trying to please him. If you want to truly please him become the best in what beings you happiness. Any skill, little one, will never bring you contentment unless it is what you want to do."

Her eyes found the rack of the training swords on the far side of the field. She loved to hunt but the swords seemed to call her name.

"Remember, not unless you want it for yourself."

He stood.

"Alright students, let's do that all over again! I want to see much better work this time!" He called out to the others who were already notching their arrows waiting for the signal. He looked back at Anath. "Now, show *yourself* what you can do."

Anath watched the old man walk down the line of students, pausing here to instruct one and halting to inspect another's bow. His words were wise, she knew, and she trusted his instruction. *What can I do?* She took a deep breath and closed her eyes.

All around her, she heard the other student's bows singing as their arrows released. Shouts and claps erupted as some favored student hit the mark or one missed, but she tried to ignore them.

Strong and sure.

Taking a deep breath, she stood tall and straight as she pulled firmly back on the cord until her hand touched her cheek.

Strong and sure, just as Turga had instructed her, she focused on the target and suddenly felt she *knew* what would happen. She could see it in her mind.

The arrow swiftly flew from its notch. Shooting swiftly, it seemed to sing as it moved through the air. From the corner of her eye, she saw her father lean forward then, watching closely, until the arrow found its mark in the target with a loud thud.

Her arrow quivered briefly in the very heart of the marker. Then, only then, she realized she had been holding her breath. Hers was the only arrow to strike the center of the target.

Other students rushed to congratulate her but she looked around for her father. He was already turned away from her heading toward where Turga stood.

Her father did not turn back to where she waited. He nodded to the instructor, spoke a few words too low for her to catch and then he turned away.

Without a word to her, he walked away and was soon lost in the crowd of people setting up for the market. Anath accepted the rowdy comments of the students but she felt strangely empty. She smiled, though, and replied to their jests with ease.

"Good shot, little one!" Turga spoke at her elbow with a laugh in his voice. "Your father was impressed."

"How can you tell?" She collected her arrows and stuffed them in the quiver. It had belonged to her Mother and around it were the strange symbols of her people: spirals, and waving lines, and other odd markings. "He never speaks or seems to see me."

Waving as someone shouted a farewell, she slung the bow and quiver over her shoulder.

"I can tell, *child*, because he gave me instructions as to your training."

She glanced up then afraid he offered some ill-timed jest. Turga's tanned and wrinkled face was alight with pleasure.

"He gave you instructions? He really said something about me?"

"He wants me to concentrate on your training. He sees in you the skills of your Mother. Yes, your father was proud. Very proud indeed." Turga ruffled her hair as he gruffly added, "As I am proud too! Although you can be such a pebble in my sandals sometimes!"

Anath cleaned her equipment and helped to clear away the weapons. Long after the others had hurried off to their homes she remained. She kept out of sight or tried to appear burdened with some task whenever anyone did see her. She wanted no comments about her delay at leaving or for anyone to note her habit of lingering as the day faded.

She hovered around the training yard, just around the edges or in the shadows, so she could be there as the new group arrived. From the village and the hills around the yard, after their duties of the day were completed, came the warriors for their time of training.

Finding her usual spot atop a large rock she huddled down on its warmth. She could not be seen in her perch but from here she had a good vantage point to observe. Digging in the leather bag at her waist she pulled out the piece of bread and the dates she saved from the morning. Getting comfortable, she settled down to watch as the warriors took the place of the students.

The warriors were men and women whose skills in fighting and strategy had already been sharpened in battle. They fulfilled one of the sacred duties of the people. She heard in her mind the droning voice of her teacher explaining it all. "The duties define us and helped us to live peacefully and be prosperous." The duties included the warrior, the hunter, the priest, the storyteller, the healer, the sages, and the crafters of wood, cloth, metal and stone.

Zeni had told her the sacred duties were like the arrows in her quiver. Each person could have many different arrows or arrows of all one kind. The gods birthed the skills in each person as they saw fit. It was the duty of the people to encourage their use and develop the skills for the benefit of all.

Her sister was learning the hunt but did not enjoy it as much as some of the children. She enjoyed more working with the healers and the priests. There was little doubt what role her sister would one day assume.

Anath had learned the skills of the hunt and knew she could feed her family or help feed her people. She had felt good learning those skills. She knew she showed promise, but seeing the lean muscled bodies moving in defense and thrust, hearing the ring of the swords as they connected, showed her there was still so much she had to learn. She wanted to learn more but dare she dream of being a warrior?

Was it to be her duty to be a hunter only? If so, why did the work of the warriors fascinate her so?

Carefully, she studied each move and each counter move, and tried to keep its picture in her head. She would copy them at home when everyone was asleep. She had to learn them; surely *then* her father would be proud of her.

The light was nearly gone and the torches burned low as Azon finished the practice steps. With a laugh, he slapped his opponent on the back.

"Go home! You fight like an infant. Run home and see if there is an equal there yet!" Tagi's wife was having their first child and his mind was far away these days.

"I was being easy on one with so much sand in your beard." Tagi mocked as he put away the weapon.

"Ah," Azon stroked his beard and nodded at the retort. "It does look a bit more like the ash in the fire pit every day."

Rontoi, her long braid, reaching to her waist, moved quickly to run her hand over the receding hairline of Tagi. "At least, he does not have the pate of an infant."

Laughing at the joke, Rontoi turned to pick up some the weapons and joined the others as they headed toward the open tent. Inside, in the amber glow of the lamps, others joined them to polish the shields and sharpen the edges of the blades. They worked swiftly, a light banter to their exchanges, but always with great care and attention for their weapons.

As they finished, they all gathered at the center of the opening near the tent. Azon speared a blade into the ground. Thrusting out bronzed and calloused hands they all clasped the hilt.

Azon felt once more the eyes on them. For several weeks, he had made note of the child who tried to hide in the shadows and watch them. It happened occasionally that children and youth would spy on the warriors as they worked the blades.

This child sat on the rocks, veiled in the shadows, as still as a deer hiding in the grasslands. Her stillness had made him curious. Children were restless creatures whose attentions soon drifted away to other things. This one was curious and patient. Turgi had told him it was the oldest daughter of Dagon.

Above them was the great dark bowl of the sky. Legend said that the darkness came from the rising of a vast forest of trees covered with silver buds. Now, the stars had begun to bloom on the great branches of the heavens. *Time to go home*, he thought, *and warm his aging bones around his fire.*

He began the chant shared by those who had chosen the skills of protection and battle. He had learned the chant as a skinny youth nearly fifty harvests ago. They had words they chanted for war, for peace, and for honor. When he breathed his last, they would lay his body on a platform. As the flames consumed his body, the entire community would beat the drum and dance. As they moved they would recite a song for his entry into the afterlife.

"Today we are warriors...
Tomorrow we will be warriors...
Until we draw our last breath –
We guard the people.
We serve the people.
The people are us

And we are the people.

Swift as a Raven we fly

With an Eagle's claw we cut;

We will be warriors.

We are family.

We are friend.

We are warrior."

Left alone by the departing warriors, Azon dunked his head into the cold water in the basin. Lifting out his head, he shook the water off and saw that the child was now gone. He used a scrap of worn mantle to wipe the excess water away. He tried to recall all he knew about the child. Her Mother had been the outsider, the strange woman, who had all the marks of a fighter scored into her every move. His thoughts already on his warm fire, Azon started down the path to his home, but he knew he would remember her.

In this harsh land, good warriors were always welcome. Although peace had been theirs for many seasons, he knew that could change in the moment it took to draw a single breath. Peace was always as fragile as mist beneath a scorching sun.

Chapter 4

"Is that her?" Asherah whispered to her sister Anath as they stood side by side on the courtyard steps a few years later. Several camels approached the home of Dagon. The tall spindle legged beast halted by the pens and a woman slid down to stand by Dagon. Together they approached the house.

The breeze was warm and tugged at Anath's straight hair and ruffled the dark curls of her little sister. Although, it was harder to think of her that way anymore; she had added height since her last birthday. She was entering the first class of archers soon and Anath would be helping to train the second class.

This was the day when her father Dagon brought his new wife to the mountain home. As they entered the courtyard, Anath realized she was nervous. She felt a hand clench her midsection and her mouth was suddenly dry. She wished to be anywhere but here. Her sister beside her appeared as cool as the stone of a cave but she was clenching her fist nervously.

Senath was a tall, willowy woman used to having her every movement followed. Like a robe of fire, her long red hair hung down her back. It fell past her hips and glowed in the light. Anath had never seen hair the color of the setting sun.

Everything about the woman was strange and exotic. The scent of flowers and moonlight trailed around her leaving images of gardens and dreams. Twelve-year-old Anath had been quickly awed by her beauty.

"Don't tell me these are your daughters?" Senath remarked seeing the girls lingering in the doorway. Her voice was musical and, from the way her father's face seemed to glow listening to her speak, it was part of her attraction.

"Come here children," her father swept his great robe from his shoulders flinging it carelessly to the floor. "Let your lovely new Mother get a good look at you."

"Where are these sons you boast of my love?" the woman smiled at her husband. "Did you dream them?"

Dagon's smiled faltered a moment. "I will be back in a moment. Hadad! Melqart!" Her father strode off down the hall calling for the boys. "Boys! Where are you children!"

As he walked away, the woman approached the two girls and circled around the duo as if they were lambs in the market place. She ruffled the head of Asherah bringing a small smile to the nervous child.

Examining Anath, she slowed down and suddenly reached out to grab her upper arm. In a firm grip, she felt the muscles and examined her arms. Anath tensed at the act but she held her tongue with great effort.

"Stand tall girl!" she barked suddenly in a sharp voice that shocked Anath. She lifted her head to glare at this...interloper into her home.

Senath merely nodded and returned the look. "Ah, so there is some small spark of spirit in this skinny body. Good!"

Long silken fingers lifted the girl's chin until she found herself staring straight into the strange green eyes of the woman. It seemed that the more she gazed into them the faster the gold specks swirled in their depth. They were like whirlpools of glistening emerald.

"Remember this child. Hear and be forewarned. No child of mine will stand with head bowed as if in fear. No! From now on, meet my eyes and always stand tall as the goddess made you."

"Yes. I will remember."

"*Mother.* You will call me Mother for that is now what I am to you both. That will be strange to you, I know. All of my husband's wives died when you were young. As if the custom of my people I will view all of you as mine." She smiled suddenly and something in it evoked a responsive grin from both girls.

"Good!" she looked to where her husband had disappeared. "Now, since my new husband has seen fit to leave me here, you will have to take me to my rooms. The journey was dirty and long. I would rest before the last meal."

Anath led the woman down the steps into the interior of the house where the halls were cool and dark, small pools of light from the lamps cast soft flickering shadows as they moved past. Carved from the rock mountain, these rooms stayed cool in the summer and warm in the winter.

Stopping before the double doors of the main bedchamber, Anath threw them open with a small flourish for the rooms were truly beautiful. Her father's last wife, Melqart's mother, had been able to bring the room to life through her gifts. A ribbon of brilliantly painted images of trees and plants circled the room just below the ceiling and the floor was a dazzling spiral mosaic of tiny colored pottery pieces and stones. The finest materials covered the wide bed shelf and soft furs softened the chill of the floor.

Senath said nothing as she slowly walked around the room. She briefly touched the gauzy bed curtains and ran her fingers over the jars of perfumed ointments on a low ebony table.

"The room is beautiful." Anath said without question. She knew it was a rare room, reflecting the gentle and imaginative woman who had lived in it for such a short time.

"Yes, it will do." Senath said as she flung open the shutters and took in the view of the white sands and the distant purple mountains. "Leave me now daughter and see that my things are carried here. If my husband returns – send him to me here."

Anath said nothing but turned to hurry back to the main hall. Footsteps echoed and the sound of voices in argument heralded the approach of her father and Hadad. Older than Anath by seven years, Hadad was now surpassing their father's height and many thought he might still be growing.

Melqart trailed along behind in his usual watchful silence. As the youngest at ten years, he often trailed in Hadad's shadow, but was as different from his brother as the moon from the sun. Where Hadad was outgoing, seeming to seek out adventures like a starving man hunted food, rail thin Melqart showed little interest in hunting and preferred to go off alone to think.

Lately, Hadad was chaffing at being kept so close to his father's side. He had been leading the trading caravans for several seasons and was no stranger to the tasks.

The trips brought him the adventure he so often craved. Now, kept closer he thought his father no longer trusted him. He also was bored and often found trouble.

"But father, I was coming." Hadad was arguing. "I was on my way even as you called. Melqart will tell you!"

"Melqart loves his brother and would say whatever needed to be said to protect your hide!" Dagon snapped off each word. "How dare you go off into the hills when you knew that I was returning with your new mother."

"She is not my Mother." Hadad muttered. He still grieved at his Mother's death and his grief often brought anger.

"Never let me hear that again," commanded his father. "The god's help you if you ever let her hear such a remark either."

"Now, both of you go and get cleaned up. You are filthy!"

As he turned to obey, it was clear he felt his father's sharp rebuke her heard her father sigh. "Anath, did you see your Mother to her rooms?"

"Yes, father. She wanted you to go to her as soon as you returned."

The look that bloomed on her father's wrinkled face made Anath turn hers away. Such a look of emotion was hard to see without feeling she had opened a door into something very private. She had seen him look that way when her Mother had spoken to him. Later, she had also seen it shared with the Mother of Melqart.

It was hard to live here in the blue shadow of Mount Cassuis. He had chosen wives of his heart too often without thought of the toll the harshness of the place might have on the women.

From stories she knew that Hadad's Mother had been a short, round limbed woman who died from fever when he was very small. She had died in a riding accident in the foothills. The next wife was Astarte, mother of Anath and Asherah. A stranger she had died of fever. Dagon had married next a tall women with raven dark hair and deep brown eyes. She had died in giving birth to young Melqart.

Now, he had brought yet another woman home as his wife.

Nearly everyone in the household worked to adjust to the newcomer in their midst. She was a successful trader's daughter from the cold northern countries. She was skilled in selling and trading. Senath was also a hunter and a poet, soon winning the hearts of the girls and Melqart.

Only Hadad remained aloof and resistant. He seemed to despise everything about her and often spoke sharp words to her or his father before storming off to ride the desert for long hours.

She seemed to understand that a young man of his years needed challenge. She mediated with Dagon on Hadad's behalf, and the young man was finally given the responsibility of training the older boys. He was also given more duties with the trading parties. For a time, the household was once more the way it had been before Melqart's mother died.

It was Senath's idea that Hadad be given a horse and she had bartered with the traders hard for just the right one for the youth. When the black horse had arrived, it was as long limbed as Hadad. It tugged at its reins, eager to be away and with its jagged white stripe down its face it seemed like captured lightening. Momentarily, the youth forgot his animosity.

"He is named Cloudrider." Senath told him.

"He is marvellous!"

"He is yours. Take good care of him and he will take care of you one day."

She set about to win the hearts of all of the children. She had encouraged Anath to be strong and courageous. Dagon listened to her words and the training in the hunting arts continued. Senath saw she was interested in learning the sword and set about to teach her.

"In my people, a woman must be able to fight alongside her mate. I learned the songs of battle as a child." She told the girl as they practiced in the early dawn. "Although I became a trader, if needed, I could still fight."

She was a brusque but caring Mother to the girls and Melqart. She was radiant the night she said they would soon have another in the family. It was never to be, however, after long happy months preparing for the new baby, Senath had died. She had struggled for many long hours, with warrior fierceness, to bring a tiny girl into the world. The child had the dark eyes of Dagon and the fiery hair of her mother. She survived the death of her mother by only minutes.

Anath thought the babe just could not bear to be parted from her mother after so many months under her heart. Missing yet another mother, Anath thought she could understand why she might have chosen to go to the afterlife instead of staying with them. In the cool of the evening, as stars began to bloom in the sky, they buried the ashes of both in the shadows of the blue mountain.

Chapter 5

Several months later, patterns of life began to reform around them all, and things settled into the too familiar cycle of training, working and lessons. An afternoon of training had dissolved as the first rain drops fell.

The rains had come early and after a torrid summer, it made exercises with lance and axe impossible for any but the most dedicated. Turga ruefully shook his head seeing the gleam in the eyes of students anxious to enjoy the cooling winds and the rains.

Anath, and her sister, Asherah, joined their friends. Soon all of the students danced around enjoying the feel of the fat drops on their faces. They even tugged old Turga into the fun.

"Go! You are all worthless urchins!" Turga waved them off. His scared face, though, crinkled in what passed for a smile.

Screeching, and calling out to one another, the older youth spilled away from the training field. Hadad and some of the older young men leaped to the back of the horses standing by the camp. They bent low over their necks and raced toward the approaching storm clouds.

Thunder boomed as they watched them ride away. Fingers of light stretched from dark clouds to earth. A gust of wind filled the air with the smell of rain and the throng hurried toward the shelter of the tents.

"Those foolish boys!" exclaimed Penne as she herded the younger students into the larger tent. "They will call down the wrath of Anu for certain with their reckless ways."

The inside of the tent was dark. The rain slapped against the tent in an uneven beat. The air was filled with the smells of leather, incense and platters of food steaming on a low table. Succulent slices of meat, fresh bread, platter of cheese, and bowls of fruit.

"Now, hurry and eat while it is still warm. Then we will gather over there on the rug and I will teach you tactics of the hunt..."

Filled with the surprising banquet and the excitement of the rain, Anath had trouble keeping her mind on the woman's words. She had been helping teach the younger ones each morning and in the afternoon learning herself. She had lessons from the history keeper, from the artisans, the priests and others representing the duties required of the people.

Thinking of duties drew her mind back to her brother. Glancing at the rain pouring down she thought of brother's decision to abandon the trading work and come home. Of late, he had seemed to be growing more bored and unsettled again. Once more he was acting very reckless of late. His quarrels with their father were an almost daily event.

From their often loud arguments, she knew Dagon had been disappointed his son seemed unwilling to settle down. The truth was Hadad seemed unwilling to take any responsibility beyond his own pleasures.

The rain had cooled the air and she pulled a cloak tightly around her shoulders. The horizon was barren of any life. It had been hours now since her brother had raced off leading the other boys.

Namu had explained to her that her brother was becoming a man and that men of his age often acted fools. Yet, she worried about her brother's strange attitude of late was something else. There seemed to be a bottomless well of hate in him. His sudden angers and his bristling attitude to everyone, but especially to their father, was a frightening thing to see. The new tension in their home was unsettling and she sensed it would cause trouble for all of them before long.

The rain was lessoning and she went outside the tent. She saw in the distance a group of riders racing back across the sodden ground. *He is still just a boy*, she thought, *and still my brother.*

"Anath, you must help me! Make him see my side of things." Her brother said to her a few days later.

It was not often Hadad begged anything of his younger sister. Anath recognized this was a sign of his desperation. He still liked to be in control and make things change to suit his desires. They sat on the shaded terrace where they had played as children. "I cannot take this place anymore!"

"You know he will not listen to me." Anath laughed. "He seldom even speaks to me! For a long time, he has not really been here, with his family."

"And when he is here, he is impossible to please."

"He has great responsibilities and he grieves Hadad…"

"I should have known you would take his side!" he hurled back at her. "Why do you do that? He treats you like a ghost as if you do not really exist. Yet, you are always trying to please him!"

"Hadad, please…"

"You are not even his! Your mother walked out of the desert carrying you in her belly." Hadad laughed but it was an ugly thing, twisted with hatred.

Anath froze at what she was hearing. If he had stabbed her in the heart she could not have felt more pain and sudden doubt.

No, she was Dagon's daughter! That was what she had always been told. What if she was not? Was that why her father was always so distant? She was not his and so he did not love her? A pain cut her deep inside and then she realized her brother still spoke his poison.

"I bet he loved that!" His face twisted into an ugly grimace but his eyes burned in glee. "Yes, imagine taking a woman only to learn she was pregnant by another man! She never spoke of where she came from or who people were. She would never talk about that! Now, I wonder why that was, *little sister*? Was he a raider or a monster? Maybe some foul god in some disguise?"

Her hand arched across his face and the impact cracked like a whip. The silence that followed was deafening as his every muscle taunted. Her hand stung but she stood tautly before him. Anath glared at the angry red patch on his face and wished she had drawn blood. She realized in sudden awareness she had routinely prepared herself for possible fight and was ready.

Strangely, Hadad, holding a hand to his cheek, was the one who backed away. Suddenly, years of living with him as brother and sister, family and companion, swamped over and she too moved back.

"I beg your forgiveness, brother." She murmured hanging her head. "I should have not struck; you are my near kin. Your words though…they dishonor my Mother. Such talk dishonors your father and you." *Was he her father?* "You know they are not true."

"You, of course, know the truth of events before your birth?"

"She lived with our people here for nearly a year before she became his bride."

"So they say." Hadad moved further away as if in the movement and the distance he could gain some level of control. "Who to ask but old women and crazy old men." He made an abortive movement as if he would apologize but then his face twisted. "No matter what the discussion, in the end it is always about him!"

"He is our father…even if what you say is…true…then by choice, if not by blood. We should honor him as such."

"What about us, Anath? What about me!" Haddad stalked around the terrace, an animal once again seeking an escape from his confinement. He shoved a clay pot with herbs off so that it shattered onto the stones of the porch. He ground a sandal into the tender plants. "Sometimes I just want to crush *him*!"

"You act a child! You must learn to control your temper. Temper is a wild beast and in self-control one masters the wildness."

Turga often said that in training. It seemed to mirror her brother in a frighteningly accurate way. Anath remembered hunting an animal once that was not sure if it wanted to fight or run away. Hadad reminded her of that creature's frantic pacing.

"I nearly killed one of the workers today." The ugly bravado was gone and for a moment she saw the brother she had known so long.

"No!" Anath leaned forward but then caught herself. He was so different lately. Who could say where such reckless actions might lead? So far his vile moods had been limited to hot words and moody silences. She glanced at the herbs crushed into the shards of the pot. "You always had a foul temper but it must be tamed."

"It is more than just temper." He sat down beside her. His face was troubled as he looked up at her. "It is like a wine or a hunger. Inaction is a prison. Freedom; I need that as much as air."

"You are free, Hadad!"

"No! I am a prisoner here. They all expect me to become him. To simply step into his life and carry on as if there was no *me*…as if I were a dream."

"Everyone knows you, brother!" His sister argued. "You are the best hunter in the valley. Who arranged the trade agreement with the Hitta and the Kelti? That was you!"

"That is not enough. Those things do not make me happy. I need change and I need to be able to move. Not be chained to a herd or a crop." A small dark fist of clouds was hurtling towards the house from the far horizon. It swelled and roiled as it moved. Jagged spikes of lightening pierced the clouds as it passed. "I am too much like that storm. I need the flash and the roar."

"After the storm, though, there is calm and peace." Anath searched for the right words to catch her brother's attention. "Can you not find both here, brother?"

He looked at her for a long moment, emotions dancing across his face, and then shook his head. He looked torn between regret and eagerness as he turned to leave her. "It is too late. I have to go away. *I have to*…"

She stood watching him ride away. She felt suddenly very sad and alone as the storm grew near. When the rain fell with a muted roar she finally gave way to the tears.

Hadad rode hard and long, Cloudrider stretched out across the miles in his steady and sure pace. He did not know how far he had come but it seemed the mountains where closer. Their cool shady heart beckoned to him. Here, he finally felt the freedom and the escape he sought so desperately.

I need change, he had told Anath, *and I need to be able to move. Not be chained to a herd or a crop. I am too much like that storm. I need the flash and the roar."*

"After the storm, though, there is calm and peace."Anath said. *"Can you not find both here, brother?"*

As he raced toward the ebony clouds, the wind kicked up and lightening shot down in brilliant sparkling fingers.

The air reverberated with thunder and Hadad lifted his head and his hands, giving an exultant cry!

Yes!

Cloudrider twisted suddenly as lightening sizzled near enough to cause the air to hiss and crackle. In fright and anger, the stallion kicked off his rider. Hadad picked himself up from the rocky ground wincing from the hard landing.

Grasping his side, he breathed deeply, and watched the horse gallop away. In minutes, the animal was a mere speck on the horizon and he was in the middle of nowhere. Turning toward the towering peaks, he began to walk.

He walked for hours and he did not see the men until it was too late to hide. He was thirsty enough to not care who they were. If they carried water, he would be out of his misery and if they killed him, it would have the same effect.

They raced up to him, strong and forbidding, their skin carved and pierced with bits of bone and metal. They carried an air of menace he felt he could almost touch.

"The sand rats come early!" called one in a growling voice as the group circled him.

"No, he is too weak for a rat." Another rode around Hadad. He examined him with a contemptuous look. "I'd call him more a gnat!

The others laughed, but the sound brought no smile to Hadad. Another rider, astride a glossy black horse, broke through the clustered group. The others grew silent and backed away. The newcomer gazed hard at Hadad. His skin was as brown as his leathers and his hair as dark as the night. Long, jagged scars slashed across his cheeks.

Hadad looked at his eyes and had to look away. He had never seen such eyes. Despite the heat he shivered. *Please, let them kill me quickly.*

"Give him water!" the man ordered. His voice was low and carried authority. Hadad recognized that tone if not the owner of the voice. Dagon had that tone with his workers and his men. Here, too, was a man used to giving commands and having those orders followed.

One of the men sprang from his horse, untied the water bladder, and handed it to Hadad.

Hot and gritty, the water was nonetheless refreshing. Hadad wiped his face and took another long drink.

"Thank you," he said handing the bladder back to the man. His voice was faint and his lips so dry they bled as he tried to move them.

"It will be evening soon." He turned his horse away and remarked to his men. "Bring him with you to the camp."

One of the men rode to Hadad and thrust a muscled arm out. Hadad hesitated only a moment before he climbed behind the man. They whole group turned to follow the one who was the obvious leader. Hadad looked back to the place on the horizon. He could not see it from here. His home, and all he knew, hid in the shaded cleft in the rocks far away in a shaded valley. He wondered if he would ever go back.

With bellows of laughter and calls to the villagers, the village warriors raced back through the streets, and up to the training camp. Anath, putting away the equipment, turned as they arrived.

The warriors and the hunters had been away from the village for some days. Their laughter and high spirits generally brought a smile to old Turga and today was no different.

As the sun began to turn the day a glowing bronze he leaned on his walking stick. He stood watching as they hefted bundles over muscular shoulders and came up the hill to the school grounds.

"Good day Turga!" The oldest one called a greeting. He was built like Hadad and Dagon, which meant he was shorter than Anath with broad shoulders and muscled legs. Azon also had a dark full beard that nearly covered his face. He sometimes laughed and said it was added protection in battle.

"You were successful in locating the metal craftsman?" Turga demanded as he eyed the bulging container on Azon's back.

"We have weapons here! They are like none seen this side of the Blue Mountains or in the entire southern desert." He laid the bundle down and proceeded to lay out a collection of swords on the blanket.

Anath was awestruck, and without thought, stooped down to examine the blades. Some were the short and heavy style she knew were good for close fighting. They were like the larger hunting knives she knew. She picked one of them up and held it aloft. She examined the skill of the metal worker who had forged such a fine piece in fire and ice.

"I see they meet with Anath's favor at least," remarked Azon with a grin.

She realized that the others had also joined them and were laying down their own bundles for Turga to inspect. Some glanced at Anath strangely. Blushing, she quickly laid the weapon back down and stepped back.

"Yes, they did," said Turga looking at her with a small frown. "See the bows are properly put away Anath. Then you are to go home. Give your father our greetings."

Nervously she bobbed her head. She scanned the faces of the others before she turned away and hurried down the path to do as Turga had commanded. *Fool!* She berated herself as she jogged down the hillside and home.

How did I dare to touch the weapons of the warriors! A child trained only to hunt. Fool! I will be cleaning slop pots until I am old for such insolence…

Chapter 6

The rains passed and the long winter season set in with a long drought. Bitter cold winds scoured down across the plains from the high mountain ranges to the north. The students continued to train, even harder than before, all through the cold days. The older student had to travel farther afield to find game. The nights in the open were harsh and uncomfortable. It seemed that when Hadad left he took with him all the warmth.

When the spring finally returned Anath was ready for her own escape. There had been nothing but hard training and the long weeks away from her home. *I need to have some ease and some relaxation,* she thought as she rubbed her bruised shoulder. Dreams of a soak in hot water rose in her mind. She turned to watch as her sister scrambled up the rocks to where she stood. "Come on, you are so slow!"

"I do not have your long legs, you horse!" Her sister stood beside her with a grin.

"No respect. You are picking up bad habits, little sister." Anath laughed, leaping across a break in the rocks and then swung down to a small ledge. Standing there, she could more easily scan the desert spilling out from the outcrop. A thin column of dust was shimmering in the sunlight and from the size, it looked to Anath as if a fairly good sized party was crossing the plain. They were too far away for her to identify them. Frowning, she realized, their weapons were at the base of the rock.

"Hurry down Asherah!" She slid down one side and jumped to the ledge below.

Her sister looked to protest but, when she too saw the sign of travelers nearing the rock formation, she said nothing. She scrambled quickly down the rock ledge behind Anath. Grasping their bows and quivers they prepared themselves. Together they watched as the strange party approached.

"Stand strong." Anath told her sister touching the knife at her belt.

"I'm afraid." Asherah whispered.

Anath smiled slightly. She noticed that for her sister being afraid obviously meant stand shoulder to shoulder, weapons ready, with her sister. Then her attention went back to the approaching party. The man in the front had seen them as they stood on the lower levels of the rocky promontory. He turned the small party toward them.

Closer now, Anath could make out the man in the lead and tensed her hands. It was Yamm.

He was tall and lean but there was nothing else to commend him. His walk was too assured, his eyes too searching, and he liked to stand too close especially when he spoke with a woman. Of late he had begun to notice that Anath and her sister were no longer the children they had once been.

Yamm was a bully who had clashed with Hadad in the market competitions each year. There was no love lost between Yamm and her family. She was certain that he would not hesitate to kidnap them or use them to cause pain to Dagon.

Despite the possibility of danger she could not violate the custom of the land. Travelers sought out those they met to share news, water, or simply a short conversation.

Anath knew she was honor bound to an encounter. Sometimes, however, those without honor would waylay and ensnare those they encountered. Such would gladly leave their bones to rot in the sun no matter what was custom.

They should not have come so far without someone or one of the dogs. If they were harmed it would be her fault.

"Do you have your knives as well?" Anath asked without taking her eyes off the approaching party.

"Yes."

"Be prepared." She stepped down from the rocks.

"For what?" Asherah asked.

"Anything."

The camp was nestled in a rugged canyon and was filled with shadows. High white stones rose like bones as if they had been swallowed by a monster. Night had crept into the camp as the stars filled the sky but it was chill and strange. Each step seemed to cut him off from his past. A harsh cry went up as the men arrived and Hadad gazed around curiously. Women cloaked in dark robes rushed to the men with goblets spilling dark wine. Others led the horses away to rub them down and feed them.

Bantering, the men clustered around the fires tossing on fresh wood so that flames, red and hungry, sprang to life. Other women began to serve the men a thick spicy stew in wooden bowls. Many of them had small bones woven into the dark strands of their hair and they made a strange music with each movement.

Hadad was surprised when a woman with long ebony locks came to him with wine and food. She averted her eyes and he noticed none of the women looked directly at any of the men. He was unused to such servile attitudes. He shook his head trying to image Anath, or any of the women of his people, waiting on him hand and foot.

As she began to brush off the dust of travel he froze. Another woman joined the first. He heard the men laughing as he gave into the strange sensation as several female hands massaged his shoulders. He gasped as someone washed his face and chest with a spice scented rag. He grinned thinking he could learn to enjoy such treatment.

Everyone relaxed after that as they ate and drained goblets of wine. Soon music from deep toned drums filled the night. The men lounged and the women continued to fill their cups and bring them more food. No children peered from the tents or chased after the heroes. The drums seemed to pound in time to his heart. He looked into his goblet and wondered what was in the wine. He spoke to the man closest to him about the lack of families.

"The children remain with the old ones." One of the men said when he asked. "What use are they when we raid?"

"Your leader. What is he called?"

"Mot. Mot, the mighty and the magnificent one!" the man laughed as he bit off a hunk of meat. Rivulets of grease streamed down his jaw but he ignored it as he ate.

"You must not believe all you hear," said a voice behind him. Hadad turned to see Mot behind him, a young woman at his side, "Dasil here will help ease the weariness from you."

The woman came closer and taking a cloth began to wipe his face, arms, and body. A strong heady scent filled his nostrils and her touch was soft.

The music sounded different now, the drums more insistent, and all around women began to dance in slow sinuous movements that stirred the blood and made breathing more difficult. An air of excitement seemed to be building all around him. The same nervous energy of horses straining at the bridle that kept them in place.

One of the women tossed something into the fire and multicolored sparks burst out. It was beautiful and he watched as a haze drifted over the area of the fire. The haze seemed almost alive as it coiled outward toward the men around the fire. An aroma filled the air reminding him of the scent on the wash cloths used earlier to refresh the men. His head felt heavy and unclear as if he had taken his fill of wine.

In supple and sinuous motions, the women all moved around the fire, long glistening brown longs peeking through the slits in their long robes. Bare feet gracefully moving to the beat. Each step accompanied by a jangle from ornaments on their ankles. The smoke reached him and he breathed deep. Something, warm and tingling, filled him with each breath. It consumed him and he could feel it flowing through his body.

Through the dancing flames, he could see the shadowy form of Mot, silently staring at the scene.

His head began to whirl then, the drums and his heart merged into one single beat. The jingle of the anklets and the flash of the sleek legs made him oblivious to anything but the moment.

The woman by his side poured him more wine and brought it to his lips. The drums began to beat more rapidly as his heart raced to keep time. He gulped down more of the wine and laughed with the others. He pulled the woman closer….

He suddenly felt like he had come home.

As she watched from the rock ledge the hazy group of travelers resolved into more discernable shapes. Closer, Anath saw the party was less forbidding than she had first feared but still dangerous looking. Several men with lances and bows followed Yamm and beyond them came several women. Anath saw they were loaded down like pack animals.

As she watched, one stumbled and one of the men slapped her across the face loudly berating her clumsiness. Anath winced at the sight; she had heard that there were some from the fringes of the sands who worshipped cruel and violent deities. Gods who did not value women. This was the first she had seen what that meant. They did not recognize a woman's strength. They were certainly not like her Mother's people.

Yamm signaled the larger party to wait and came towards them with a small group of men. He was a tall muscular man with a hard face and bold eyes. Despite his apparent male strength, there was also evidence of vanity in his nature by the gold bracelets he wore and the fine green cloth wrapped around his waist.

A simple warrior or a traveler would not wear those. They were the spoils of a thief. They were worn simply to prove his ability to raid and steal from anyone he encountered.

He came near enough to eye the two girls as they stood at the foot of the pile of large rocks. He smiled in a way that made Anath wary; he was like the cat enjoying the idea of some play with a mouse.

"Hadad's little sisters!" he called as stopped. His eyes moved over each of the girls in a way that was insulting. Anath felt a sudden desire to cleanse herself. "You grow lovelier each time I see you."

He came close enough that she had to lift her eyes. He smelled of sweat and exotic spices she could not name. He seemed to inhale her like an animal. At last, he turned toward Asherah and lingered even longer on the younger girl's face. He appeared intrigued, by the way the wind rustled the tight ringlets of the younger sister's dark hair. "My friend Hadad must offer me his hospitality. A true friend would want me to know his family better."

"I am sure, *my father* would welcome the opportunity to greet you," Anath told him.

He laughed at her words. His eyes continued to linger on Asherah's form in a manner that was making her sister uncomfortable.

He darted a look back at her, "Your eyes Anath, reveal that such a welcome would likely be a knife to my throat, were you Dagon or Hadad."

He stepped forward suddenly and the younger girl retreated instinctively. Anath knew that had been an error as his eyes flashed suddenly to her sister's face. He thought he had the upper hand and her sister's fear pleased him. Watching him she saw his features twisted in a look of such naked hunger she nearly gasped. Suddenly she realized, he wanted her sister in the way a man took a woman. Her sister was little more than a child but, from a man as vile as Yamm, she was in great danger.

In that second everything changed. They were facing a greater threat in this man than any wild sand cat. He moved toward her sister in such a way that Anath knew instinctively he sought to put himself between the two girls.

Out of the corner of her eye she saw one of his men move slightly. Intuitively, Anath stepped forward blocking Yamm's move. One of her hands clearly and casually resting on the hilt of the knife in her belt.

Her sister moved as well pulling her knife free. The big man swung around with a snarl, raised his fist, but her blade sliced into the fleshly part of his arm before he moved very far.

In the blink of an eye, the scene had changed from casual threat to one of lethal danger. The very air around them seemed to crackle as the drama unfolded.

Hadad woke the next morning, his head aching, and his eyes wary of the sunlight. He lay sprawled on a carpet in a large black tent. Others, men and women, lay littered across the floor and the space reeked of the odd spices that had filled the air, stale sweat and wine. He had no memory of the night past the time at the fire and the dancing.

He wanted nothing so much as some cold water and some fresh air, but as he tried to climb to his feet, he staggered. He felt an urge to heave but stumbled toward the opening. Wincing as the harsh glare of the sunlight hit his eyes, he drew a deep breath, and felt the bile settle.

Near the entrance was a bladder of water and he hefted it to his mouth. It was hot but it would do to clear his mind of the wine.

The scene was far different from the night before. Women were busy at work over cook pots and tending the animals. From somewhere children ran about in play and older ones did their chores. They must have had another camp nearby. He shook his head trying to recall all they had told him last night. It was still confused in his memory.

"I see you have shaken off sleep. I hate sleep it is a waste but necessary." Mot had walked up behind him as he watched the children. "Come, I have fresh water in my tent. We must talk, Hadad, son of Dagon."

Chapter 7

"Back!" Anath hissed and Yamm locked his coal black eyes with her vivid blue ones. She leaned toward him to show she had no fear of him.

His only response was a growl. It rose animal like from deep in his chest. A small ribbon of blood was creeping down his arm and his eyes were deep pools of livid hate.

An odd murkiness grew in the air around them, as if a dark fog had arisen, and they seemed to be in a shadow. Anath did not take her eyes from Yamm as the shade darkened where they stood. Soon it was clear again. A cloud in a clear sky or a portent? *Focus,* she urged herself. She assumed the fighting stance she had been taught. She waited, wary and alert, all the while keeping Yamm always in her view.

Anath realized she felt odd and was suddenly aware of many things at once. She knew the man creeping towards them had halted. She knew too that Asherah had her blade out and stood ready. Quickly, her mind was reviewing every lesson and every tactic she had ever learned or heard the others discuss.

The shadowy fog was back and seemed to wrap itself around Yamm. Eddies of something vile, cold like deepest winter, reached out to touch her and she shrank back.

Then something strange happened.

It was as if someone else stepped into her skin and into her very bones. She shivered at the sensation. A burning awareness ran through her swiftly, brilliant and hot, like a bolt of lightning. She felt an odd new strength, a wild daring even, and she suddenly knew what she must do.

"Animal!" she spat out the word. She looked him in the face and moved in closer. "You are little more than an animal. Get back now, before I slit you from side to side."

The blade in her hand glinted in the sun.

Anath leaned in with it until she was inches away from the man.

The other men were pressing forward as if they would overtake her. Yamm looked into Anath's eyes and then impatiently waved the men back. Backing away several paces from her he paused. He pointed to Asherah with a smile that was all audacity. "You little one, I will see again and very soon. I promise that you will never forget that meeting!"

Holding his cut arm, he spun around toward Anath. "And I will make you pay for this!"

"Why wait? Come, let us make the knives sing now!"

The others now sensed something was different and they held back. They were used to cowering victims and this woman was not afraid.

His men backed away. One spoke: "We must go! He will not wait for us. We have dallied too long as it is."

Yamm hesitated. It was obvious he was torn between his desire to carve retribution out of her skin and the need to keep his meeting.

The party moved away with Yamm now leading the way with long, angry strides. Asherah slumped down into the hot sand.

"What were you thinking? He could have killed you...us." She stared at her sister. "Without even trying he could have skinned us alive."

Anath took a deep, somewhat ragged breath, and slipped her knife back into its sheath on her belt. She realized she had not breathed for some time. "I don't know...."

Staggering slightly she realized what she had done. "It was as if someone else was inside me. I felt as if I could do anything."

Whatever force had motivated her had now gone and she felt as weak as a newborn. She watched the group now fading into the haze of the sun on the horizon. Then she slumped down to join her sister on the sand.

Asherah took her hand and squeezed it, "It was brave, though. Father would have been proud. You should have seen yourself."

"Turga would have railed at me. I had no balance. I let anger and fear control me. I –."

"You saved *us*." Her sister broke in softly halting her rant. "He meant us harm; he meant me harm. I had visions of him bundling me off with them to carry loads of blankets and pots!"

"That would never happen. Nobody can make you work!" Anath laughed as her sister punched her shoulder. Quickly though she explained about the strange force that had seemed to guide her in the confrontation.

"Perhaps, it is a thing of our Mother's people." Her sister responded after a moment. "It was right, extremely dangerous, but right. He did mean us harm, sister. You know that is the truth. If you had not faced him that way we might both be dead."

"Yes, he did mean us harm." Anath agreed. "I am afraid that I will regret he did not die."

"Yes, with men like Yamm," her sister said softly, "he won't forgive or forget."

Turga looked up from the children he was putting through their paces with the axe. The day was pleasant but he saw clouds on the horizon that hinted at a change in the weather. He grimaced as he moved. His old bones did not move as easy as they had once.

In the distance, he saw Anath leading an older group as they danced with the knife. It had been six years since the young child had first come to learn.

Now, she was nearly as tall as any man in the village and her skills had grown apace with her stature. He knew she had already begged Sama to teach her the sword and his early reports were that she had natural skills.

"She is good with the children." Dagon had come up to stand at his side. The man's hair was now totally silver, although he still had the strength and skills of a young man.

"I wish I had a dozen like her! Especially since every trading caravan brings worrying tales of the bandits over the mountains."

"The cold will keep them on their side."

"I hear the high passes are thawing early and quite heavily this year." Turga said. "They will come."

Dagon nodded. "Yes, they probably will. It will not be the first threat we have faced or the last. There are always vermin in every field."

They watched the students for a moment.

"Did you send for the bow?" Dagon asked finally. "Anath's birthing day comes soon."

"It should be on the next caravan at the new moon." Turga chuckled. "Old Tal will bring it himself."

"Tal, that old fool, I have not seen him in years! I thought he was growing fat and lazy on the coast?"

"His family grew but not his purse. He says he will retire again as soon as the purse exceeds his children."

"Hopefully, that will be after this trip."

Anath was polishing the last of the shields and the swords in the weapons room when a sound announced someone was behind her. She turned to see her brother Melqart. It suddenly struck her how tall he had become. He had become a man without her really noticing and that shamed her. She did not see him often because of her training but also because he followed their father around learning how Dagon worked. The quiet boy who loved being alone as a child had found an affinity with the outdoors.

He loved the idea of farming, of tending flocks, and growing fields of grain. In his youngest child, Dagon finally had someone to take over the tasks and who would willingly learn the duties he had carried for so long. He was still very thin and had the dark looks of his Mother. His eyes and smile were still warm and gentle.

"Melqart, it is good to see you." Anath stopped and gave him a long look. "You look well and healthy.'

"Yes, I am." He answered and then looked around as if unsure where to begin.

"What is it?" Anath asked. "You obviously have something on your mind."

"It is Kama. She – I..." He frowned at his inability to be clear before he blurted out, "We want to marry."

Anath forced herself to keep from laughing at the young man and his struggle to state what almost all knew. The growing attraction of the pair had been like a bonfire on a dark night. Anath decided to take pity.

"Do you want me to go with you when you speak to her father and mother?" Anath asked him.

"Would you please? I seem to be unable to speak when I am with them."

"Of course, but I am surprised you did not ask Asherah."

"I did," he admitted. "She refused because of Kama's brother Rair. She is afraid he will get ideas."

Anath chuckled. "Well, second choice or not, I will go with you to assure her family their daughter could not do any better."

"Thank you, Anath." He relaxed and for a moment, she glimpsed the small quiet boy she had known once many years ago.

Suddenly she yearned for those old days. Running freely through fields or climbing over rocks in play. How swiftly had they moved on from those simple days of their childhood? Once all that occupied their thought had been playing games and escaping their endless lessons. Now, most of her friends were busy learning their trade or study a craft. When was the last time she had played?

Something else was clear to her. As happy as she was for her young brother, and she loved seeing his bright smile, she sensed there was portent in the moment. A heavy significance hung in the air and caused the moment to take on a strange clarity. Something told her she must remember this moment; it was special.

The wedding of Melqart and Kama was a festive event bringing out the entire village and many people from communities that were more isolated. The food was plentiful and the wine unending as the celebrations went on for days with dancing, stories, games, racing, competitions, and eating.

Traders had come bearing gifts for the couple. They did not ignore the opportunity and set up their wares to catch the eyes of all those who had come to wish the couple a happy future. Soon their bright stalls added to the colorful celebrations.

Dagon had built a small house near the farm. The couple would move into it after the rituals. It was near the farm and so it was near enough to enjoy their company but provided them with privacy as they set up their household. Dagon's house was a different place these days with so many of the children living elsewhere.

Zeni was still there, growing frailer with the passing years, but still full of life. She was already eager to care for the babies Kama would bring into the family. No one mentioned the absence of Hadad, especially Zeni, who had helped raise the boy.

She hinted strongly whenever she saw Anath or Asherah that they too should think of husbands. When she broached the topic within their hearing at the festivities, Anath said nothing and Asherah merely blushed. Zeni scooted them away back to the fun with a gleam in her old eyes.

The last evening the fires burned high and bright in the darkness. The music was loud and made people want to dance. Anath, however, could not shake off the strange heaviness she had felt earlier. It came back strongly as she listened to the laughter around her. Even the music had a strange intensity, as if knowing the instruments would be silent for a long time. Though the wine flowed freely and people laughed and frolicked like children. She could not shake the sense of foreboding.

Late in the evening, as moon rode high in the night sky, a group of young men, drunken and in high spirits, roared through the village and disappeared into the dark of the desert. Hadad was with them. Although he smiled and laughed in reply to the many greetings, there was an aura about him that was odd, and it made her uneasy. Maybe it was the dark leather and clothes he wore. He looked older and a harsher man. He was less the youth who had begged her to help him so long ago in the courtyard.

He greeted their father but something did not seem natural. He appeared to be acting a part as he gave his greetings to his father and the family. As he smiled and bantered with his friends, he gave the appearance of being the same fun loving and exuberant boy he had been before he disappeared for those long months. She sensed in him something wrong.

The night was late and the people dispersing to their homes when Anath saw what she thought was the figure of Hadad disappearing into the night. Frowning, she thought there was something furtive in his movements. He looked like a man with something to hide.

Five days later, long after the last of the marriage feast had been cleared away and life had fallen back into its familiar rhythm, Hadad slipped into Dagon's house in the late hours. Wearily he fell across his pallet in his chamber and slept deeply, until the door opened with a thud and sudden brilliant light streamed in.

"Go away!" He moaned rolling away, shading his eyes with an arm. "The light hurts."

A kick in his side sent him upright with a scowl. The tip of a blade just touched his neck.

"You disappear for months. Your horse returns without you. We search for days and then you just appear! Then you slink off into the dark again. Then, like some rat, you sneak back in the middle of the night!"

Anath's anger was slow to show but once it came to life…

Hadad did not move. "Sister, I was recovering from a fall from Cloudrider –."

"For months? It has been five days since the marriage feast. Your horse smells of flowers! Did you have wine in your water bag? You stink of that and more!" Anath leaned toward him, her bright blue eyes, so strange like her mysterious Mother, mere inches from his face. "You lie! You do that again and I will let Nore practice his tanning skills on your sorry hide!"

Angrily he jumped to his feet as she turned away. "Don't tell me what to do, woman!" He faced her, and she was struck by the suddenly aggressive size of him. He was as menacing in his way as Yamm had been on that rocky outcrop. Hatred shone in his eyes as he glared at her. The change in him was not her imagination. He had grown to manhood but not under the tutelage of Dagon.

He had called her *woman* in that tone she had heard the outlier tribes using. The ones who kicked their women and used them like pack animals.

"If you act the child, Hadad, why should I not treat you as one?"

Growling, he reached out, muscular arms grabbing her shoulders. With one swift move Anath turned on him, lifted his arm, and sent him sprawling to the ground.

"While you have been busy being gone, moody, playing games, riding the countryside or doing whatever you have been doing, some of us have been working!"

"I see." Hadad said as he scooted away from his sister. He had gained some control and presented her with the same artificial smile she had noted on him earlier. It did not reach his eyes. She had seen a crooked trader once with that same smile. She knew he lied with every breath. Why did Hadad feel he had to lie to all of them?

"The next I know Asherah will box my ears!"

"Give her cause and it's likely!"

Hadad got to his feet, maintaining a wary distance, obviously cautious of this new aspect of Anath. Much had changed while he learned at the feet of Mot. Apparently the children he had left in his old home had grown. Briefly he missed the past but he had a greater role to play in his new life. He had been surprised because he had not given enough thought to matters. Such carelessness might mean he would fail. The cost was too high for that. Mot had taught him much over the months and that was one of the first lessons.

He thought quickly trying to see how he might adjust plans to avoid any further surprises. His allegiance was to Mot and the cost of failure too great. He had no family. No friends. Only Mot.

"I am so sorry, sister, and beg your forgiveness."

"You once begged my help and then did all you could do make such help impossible." Anath spat out at him as she strode to the door. She stopped and looked back at him. "Give me cause to feel shamed again brother and I *will* make you sorry."

The sinuous line of the distant caravan appeared like a thin spider creeping across the desert. The white sands wavered and eddied under the searing sun before revealing tall pale camels and the white robed traders of the desert people.

Yamm squatted down until he blended into the shade of the brown rocks thrusting out of the ground around him. His men did likewise.

He knew the traders were headed for the southern lands and then would return to the lands closer to the sea. They carried fine cloth, exotic spices, food and other riches.

None of that concerned Yamm. There was only one reason why Yamm wanted this particular caravan. Dagon had ordered a special bow for his daughter Anath. A warrior people in the far northern lands had made the bow. In a place where they said trees grew mountain high. He doubted that was true. *A craftsman's wild boasting to insure a sale,* he thought.

Yamm gripped his lance remembering the feel of her blade pricking his skin. The scar had healed long ago but the shame still burned bright. She would pay, he had promised. A finely crafted bow seemed an excellent start...

Chapter 8

Anath, with the other hunters, ignored the quarry they had trailed so far and raced to the smoking remains near the oasis. Knowing the caravan was expected, a spotter had raised the alarm as the black smoke covered the rising sun.

Weapons at the ready, people all across the plain had rushed to the watering hole. They only slowed as they saw the smoldering remains of the trader camp.

Anath had seen many things in her life but never seen dead men slaughtered like animals. Now she looked around at the carnage and felt her stomach heave.

Dagon had ridden across the sands with a half dozen warriors. One of the men called out that one of the party was still alive. Her father hurried to the fallen figure. Anath recognized the figure as the old trader who specialized in healing potions. It was clear he would soon be beyond the magic herbs.

"Anaz! What happened?"

"Dagon…"

"Yes, old friend. Tell us, who attacked you?"

"Yamm."

"Why?"

"He said he wanted to pay Anath for a slight." The old man coughed up red blood. "It was why he left me alive. So that it would be known why he attacked."

"Rest easy old friend. Save your strength for the healers."

"Careful, Dagon, that one is mad. He killed with too much eagerness."

"Easy now. You rest."

"The grave is my rest." The man's eyes drifted over to where Anath stood. The man seemed to hear something far away. He beckoned to the girl.

He looked at her and smiled. He spoke as if in a trance. "You are the one," he said as she stooped down.

"Yes, it is all my fault."

"No, *you are the one*." Anath decided he rambled in his pain but then he grabbed her wrist. "Death follows him! Be careful of the death that follows him."

"Anath, perhaps you should go - ," began Dagon.

"No! She is the one who walks -." A cough sent the man flat on his back. His grip tightened on her, the eyes were sharper and intent. "It all changes now..." he whispered as his eyes seemed to glaze over and his soul left his body.

Anath stumbled away from the man's body, his words echoing in her mind, and a tightness in her chest. She had a feverish need to get away from the smell of the dead bodies. They filled the air; smoking and burning, like dozens of campfires throughout the oasis, they scarred the earth.

Suddenly the enormity of the scene made her feel as if her skin was too tight on her body. If she stayed in place she would burst into flames herself. She saw a group of hunters searching for the trail of the marauders.

As she reached the cluster of men, a cry went up. Everyone's attention was drawn to a section of one of the trails heading off into the desert.

"I have seen these before!" one of the men shouted.

As others examined the tracks, Anath recognized the trail as well. Anyone who had tracked lost herds knew those tracks since they so often had been driving the lost herds away. They warriors hurried over once they saw the group preparing to set off. They scowled on seeing the familiar prints.

"Yamm!" One of the men said as he spat into the sand. As one they all turned to stare at the burning oasis and then set off across the tawny sands at a trot.

"You can't do this Anath!" Asherah cried hoarsely, as she caught up with her sister. "Come back and leave it the warriors."

"This was all my fault! If it is Yamm, then it could have been altered if I had handled things differently that day! Or just done things better."

"You mean if you had killed him then."

"Yes!" It was stark but true. The image of those bodies was all too clear in her mind.

"Anath, you can't blame Yamm's attack on anything but him!"

"No! It was my fault. I mishandled it. I know what I must do, now." She grasped her sister's arm. "I love you. You are my other half, but go back home now. You will be safe in the village. Go back there and wait for us."

She turned away and hurried to catch up with the warriors.

Yamm had not attempted to hide his trail. Something was just not right about this. Yamm did not have an abundance of courage. His daring was in the raid and not the battle. She stopped suddenly. He wanted them to follow his trail. Why? He wasn't on it that was why. She knew it as surely as her own name. She brought up her knife and looked around frowning.

She searched the scene and knew that the path he left was one that provoked the others to chase him. Clear and distinct the tracks led off to hint at where he was and what he planned.

The shopkeepers and farmers roared after the thief. "Wait!" she called out but the others hurried past eager to be in the chase. The warriors who had paused ahead heard her and trotted down to where she stood.

The others kept passing her following the track. "What is it that holds you back?" One of the shopkeepers asked with a laugh as he passed. "Too early in the morning for a real hunt?"

The other villagers added their own barbs as they passed. They were so eager to flush out their human quarry they gave no thought to the noise they were making as they harried their prey.

Some paused but most of the others merely hurried past her too impatient to find the killers to give any thought to her. "Wait! It is a trap! We must go back."

"Go back?" One of the young men asked. "If Dagon's daughter cannot stomach a fight, go back to your sewing!"

One of the warriors, climbing up from below, turned his lance to halt the warriors who followed him. "She's right! A child could follow this path." He looked toward the line of villagers disappearing up the hillside and frowned. "Apparently that is just what some people are today."

Anath concentrated on what she remembered of hunting this region, of the terrain, where they were now, and where the trail led. All of her senses seemed so aware and sharp. Once more, she responded to some interior prompting.

"He's headed back to the village," she said, pointing to the rocks before turning to the tracks in the sand. "These are misdirection. These tracks only lead us away on a pointless chase."

She spun around and loped across toward an outcrop in the distance. She pointed: "There's a shortcut back down to the houses. This way!"

The warriors did not hesitate and quickly followed the young girl. Some of the villagers peeled off to follow the warriors. Most simply ignored them all and continued following the trail up the hillside.

Anath ran swiftly across rocky outcrops until she reached the edge of the larger boulders. She slipped through an opening that slanted downwards. As children they had so often played and hunted here. Moving surely she took the lead as the warriors followed.

Finally, they could see the village a short span ahead. Anath stooped down into the cover of the embankment and they peered over the rocks.

Anath searched the landscape and then found a small band approaching the village from the eastern side. They were keeping low and using what cover they could find. It was clear they would use the glare of the rising sun to disguise their advance. They crept through the low shrubs on that side of the rock face to hide.

She remembered the hunger in Yamm's eyes as he spoke of her sister. She had sent Anath home. She had sent her right into Yamm's trap.

"You were right." A gruff voice spoke in low approving tones near her ear.

She glanced at the warrior who had halted the others to follow her lead. He was an older man but lean and wiry. She thought his name was 'Eth.

"You followed, yet you were not certain of that?"

"It seemed right." He replied with a slight shrug. "And the signs were all wrong as you said."

"We can't surprise them –," she saw the long bow strapped to the back of one. The gift intended for her, she had no doubt. "Trapped, they will never back down."

Two of the warriors who had joined them laughed. The sound was like the low rumbles of distant thunder.

"Girl, we don't want them to back down!"

"Or, run away!" One of the others said with a broad grin.

They all stood now, divesting themselves of the hindrances of cloaks and tunics. Each one preparing bows or checking their swords. One held out a hand to help her to her feet. "You are welcome to fight with us little sister!"

He stabbed his sword into the sand and one by one, each man gripped the handle. They looked at her and she reached into the group to add her hand to those clasping the hilt.

"Together we live -."

"Together we fight -."

Anath recognized the warrior prayer and joined in for the last refrain.

"Together – this day!"

The warriors quickly moved to heft their own weapons again and sprinted across the sand. Their long legs carrying them swiftly and in a deathly silence. Frightening cries reverberated from the rocks, birds scattered in noisy chorus, and the sun burns hot on her shoulders as she hurried. Something fierce bloomed to life in her then, and with a cry, she sped after the others.

As she reached them she found herself in the midst of a battle. Thwarted, Yamm and his men had halted to confront the newcomers. Spinning awkwardly they challenged the fighters and the air was filled with the clang of metal.

Anath ran straight toward Yamm and was unprepared for his rapid turn. She felt the gust of air as his sword thrust out toward her side. He missed her flesh by mere inches and he quickly moved in to take his advantage. The bole of his lance slapped the side of her head. The blow snapped her back sending her sprawling. Twisting sharply out of the way, she sprang back to her feet. She clutched her knife in one hand and pulled a smaller one from her boot.

She had to focus.

Her head hurt and she had scraped her leg open when she had fallen. She had to go on the assault or risk death. Grabbing her knife, she launched herself at him and heard a satisfying thud as she connected. He tried to turn and block her but he had been too late.

Her knife sank deeply into his chest. Cursing, he knocked her back to the ground. She clutched the knife and scrambled to her feet. Blood ran down one side of his bare chest in thick wet ribbons. With a roar, he rushed her with his bare hands. She had to think fast. She pulled the short sword from her belt and stood poised with a blade in each hand. Her mistakes from her earlier encounter came back. She had to remain calm. Emotionless. Remember the lessons.

Dropping swiftly to one knee and her fist holding the long knife shot out to jab into his midsection. Using the motion to brace herself, she brought up the other blade and, propelling his body backwards, cut deeply across his throat.

His body jerked back, one hand going to his neck, trying to catch his life blood. His eyes wide in surprise, he struggled briefly, and then he staggered back.

"That is for old Anaz," she whispered.

He fell to his knees, clutching his ruptured throat. The last of his life slipping from between his fingers with as much speed as it had flown from his many victims.

She had taken a life.

She took a step back, retreating from this sudden new reality.

Sudden exhaustion had her wanting to sink to her knees in the dirt. She had to stay standing! She had to help the others!

Catching her breath, she struggling to stand, and knives ready, she searched the field. Around her, the sounds of the battle had already grown quiet as the others found and dealt with the other killers.

Her muscles hurt and she felt the bruises forming. She held up the knives in her hands. They glistened. Yamm's blood anointing them and she felt nausea rise anew. Then she thought of the people in the caravan. The memory of their mutilated bodies littering the sand made her weakness fade. They had been gentle people. They had never hurt anyone in all of their travels across the countryside.

Anaz would never sell his silken scarves again…

Then there was a strange silence all around her. It was done, and in the fierce sunlight, she shivered, and bowed her head.

The warriors found her there. She looked up into their eyes and saw her own soul reflected there. They understood as only ones covered in the dirt and gore of battle could.

"Come. Our work is done here, little sister."

"She is little sister no more!" Eth said as he joined them. He looked around at the debris of the battle on all sides of the group. "She is now a warrior. She has earned that title today."

Turning away, she saw the others from the oasis now stood on the outcrop. Turga and her father were there surveying the work of the small band. They were far away but she saw Turga nod at something. Her father, in his usual way, merely stared.

Turning, she strode to where Yamm's body sprawled in the dirt and picked up the bow.

She looked at it for a long time, thinking about choices and decisions, and where those trails led. Suddenly, she thrust it high above her head so all could see, especially those where her father stood, and then turned to trot after the other warriors as they headed toward the village.

Anaz had been right; today it had all changed.

Chapter 9

As they neared the village, the evening fires softened the cold of the evening. Some of the warriors and hunters had followed the other tracks. They had come back leading the pack animals piled high with the goods raided from Anaz. The tale of day's battle was shared as each new group returned and with each telling Anath grew more accustomed to being a warrior.

The sense of relief had left people in a mood to celebrate life and safety. Some had run ahead as they headed home. A cluster of men and women had surrounded them with fresh water when they returned.

One shy youth, who nearly stumbled over his own feet, hastened to serve her especially. She drank deeply, feeling some of the strain of the day fade away. Cloths with cool water and fragrant oils washed away the blood and dirt. Soon the smell of roasting meat made her realize she was hungry and had not eaten since the night before. Food and warm spiced wine began to make her feel human again.

The people herded the warriors to the side of a great bonfire as people began to join them at the blaze. The drummers and the singers soon had laughing youths running about the glowing flames. Dancing forms, hidden in skins and masks, soon joined them. The music and the laughter were infectious. She laughed as one form entreated her. She was pulled to her feet with the warriors urging on in great amusement.

The wine has gone to my head, she thought laughing but also with sudden rebellion. *Why not?* Today had been important.

She had been working so hard and learning everything she could about… so many things. She had thought some unnecessary until the day's events proved them valuable. Today she had proven she had learned important things. She knew they were very important, but the wine was strong, it made her memory a bit hazy. *Important things…*

A young man smiled at her from across the leaping flames, his body glistening in the hot glow, and she smiled. She remembered seeing him on the practice field. He had beautiful eyes.

He motioned for her to join him by the fire. Soon, she lost herself in the beat of the drums and the eager mood around her. Important lessons and more practice could wait for one night.

He did have such lovely eyes…

When at last she found her bed, sleep came quickly and with it more strange dreams. All around her was a black and silent space without definition. The place was darker than any night she had ever seen. She walked on in this murkiness but could not tell if she walked on ground or floor. Her ears felt stuffed with wool and the lack of sound made her flesh crawl. There was an odd reality to this dream. *If I am dreaming.* The last she remembered was the music and the dancing around the fire. *Where am I now?*

Ahead a light, a tiny speck of bright appeared and dancing through the darkness, it came towards her. Mere feet away it stilled and pulsed in front of her. It flexed to become a glowing form no larger than a child.

She felt a tug as unseen hands pulled her and she began to follow. Silently she walked with the light staying just ahead of her. Abruptly the darkness shifted and she was in a corridor. It reminded her of a cave but it was unlike any cave she had ever seen. Down the walls veins of shimmering colors flowed like oil cascading down their surface. They spilled across the walls in a strange rivulets of flame. Azure mixed with white and touched with yellow to form the lines stretched across the walls and floor in pulsing flows. They sparkled as the stars reflected in a pool at midnight.

She reached out, touched a wall, and felt nothing but the rough texture of cold rock. Withdrawing her hand, though, she was amazed to see the same sparkling essence lingering on her flesh. It faded in moments leaving her skin glowing palely in the strange light.

This was a strange and very special dream. Since childhood she had known dreams could be portents. It was a gift their Mother had given them. She had died too soon to explain all she knew about them or how they were used. The sisters had often talked of their dreams as children. That early experience, as bizarre as some of them had been was nothing compared to what she was experiencing now. This was something unique.

Whoever her mother's people had been they had talents far beyond any known to the people of Dagon. This one was too strange and foreign and she wondered why it came to her now?

"Where am I?" she called out. "Why am I here?" Her voice rang through the corridors but seemed flat and muffled.

Walking on down the cave path she observed more details but understood nothing of what she saw. Carved into the side of one wall was an entry and it was bolted shut. An opening was cut into the hard substance of the door. She hesitated but when she pulled up the flap, she saw a scene of such magnificence she wanted to weep.

As far as she could see there was lush green landscape. Tall leafy trees twisting in a light breeze. A sparkling silver river was weaving its way across a bright shaggy meadow. Plump clouds sailed in the blue skies. She tugged at the door latch but the door did not budge.

Reluctantly, she moved further down the hallway looking for other doors. After walking what seemed hours, she saw another door, and hurried to lift the latch. Once glance had her screaming and she slammed the small door closed. Shaken, she reeled back to hug the wall of the tunnel opposite the door. Gasping for breath, her heart pounding, she clung to the rock wall as images of skinned flesh and kettles warred with worse. Nausea rose, broiling and bitter, and she emptied her stomach onto the cave floor.

She wrestled a mad desire to rip out her eyes for having seen such horrors. Worse, whatever was in that place called to her, pleaded with her to come to where it waited amid those nightmares. Part of her wanted, needed, to join whatever that creature was, in that...place.

She could hear it now, scratching frantically at the door, seeking a crack into which it could slip one of those claw like extremities. A low murmur sought to reach her. It was like a field rat pawing for a way into a warm barn. Gnawing. Her eyes shot to the edges of the entry to see if a hole was forming. The firm substance of the barrier door did not budge or bend. Had it weakened, burst open, and allowed that thing to escape...

She bent over retching uncontrollably again and sagged against the glowing walls.

The low babbling sound, like a thousand voices whispering, began anew. "Be silent!" she shouted but the sense that something nibbled at the door came again. "No!"

She pushed herself away from the walls as the silence became apparent. "Where am I?" she screamed at last. She straightened and looked around.

Stumbling a little now, less enamored by this place than she had been just moments before, she moved further down the darkly glowing corridor. She was trotting now, the longer the hallway opened, and she was consumed with just finding a way out of the place.

She passed dark shadow filled corridors that branched off and she sensed they too were lined with the endless doors. She seemed to hear an echo of something from far away but then it disappeared. They remained dark and silent.

The small glowing orb of light blinked on again just ahead of her in the shining hallway. She followed, nearly stumbling to the ground in her haste. So much for the brave warrior, she thought in disgust, as she stiffened her spine. A part of her wanted to get out of this horrific place but another part was curious as to the reason for this dream. If she herded her fears and followed that orb of light, well, maybe then she would learn. *I will know the meaning of this dream...*

The dream spit her out like a sour grape and, surprised, she sat up in the darkened tent. Around her were the sounds of others in various stages of sleep. *It was just a dream then*, she thought sagging back down into her blankets. *Just a strange dream...just a dream.*

Dawn lightened the sky to peach as Anath walked to a rock on a small hillside and sat down. She had crept out her bed while it was still dark. She had been careful not to waken Asherah where she lay huddled beneath a cloak Anath had never seen before. She suspected her sister had been gambling again. Perhaps a wile trader had talked her into parting with her hard earned coins.

Sleep and the moonlight kisses had helped ease the aches of the fight. They would do little for her other activities of the night. She knew she would soon feel every cup of wine if she did not get some fresh air. She vowed to never drink so much again. Look at the nightmares they had given to her. *That was what they had to be. Just strange dreams caused by too much wine. That was what it had to be*. The mountains in the distance were deepest wine color. As always, they appeared mysterious and threatening. She thought of those strange caverns of her dreams. Despite the promise of a bright day her thoughts were dark.

An image of horrors in her dream flashed through her memory and she tasted again the bitter bile. The wine had to have given her those strange dreams. She would never drink another drop! She needed a clear head today to consider all that had happened and what her future might now hold.

At one time, her life had been very ordinary and even simple. As the daughter of Dagon, she would learn the skills of the hunter and the farmer. Eventually, she would marry some genial man and produce children to help with the herds and care for her in her old age.

All that changed yesterday.

She knew this in her heart as surely as she knew the sun would rise over those shadowy mountains. She had sought the battle as much as she had danced the fight. A part of her had known as she followed Yamm's trail that hunting and farming were not for her. Something had awakened in her that made it clear she would never be happy as a farmer.

Now, she knew what she must do. Dagon may not be pleased but it was her life and her decision.

Soft, warm sunlight was spilling over the village streets as she carried her hunting lance to the training grounds. Small clusters of students, mostly the younger ones, were going through their paces. Here and there an older student, probably nursing a sore head, stood around visiting with others as they waited for their training to start.

Anath headed beyond the practice fields to the weapons building. In the atrium of the building sat a shrine and there she raised the lance to thank the great goddess of her mother's people for her safety in the fight. Then she thanked her father's gods for their protection.

Finally, she placed the weapon on the rack on the other wall. On racks in the center of the room she selected a short sword and a small shield. She hefted them, getting used to their shape, feeling their weight and liking how they fit her hands.

"You have chosen then?" asked Turga as he entered the room.

"Yes." She said looking at the weapons in her hands. "I am now a warrior and not a hunter."

"A good fighter is both of those things. A good warrior must be able to defend, but often, must be willing to hunt a different prey."

"I know."

"Sometimes, like yesterday, the battle must be sought, the beast must be hunted down. Sometimes, even the boredom of peace must be endured."

"I do not remember hearing that in any of the songs."

"A secret of the guild. We have known peace a long time and some things are forgotten." Turga ran a finger down the smooth leather of a shield. "A warrior must always be able to do that which is necessary. Even when it is the boring work of planting or herding animals. They do not retire from their work like those in the other duties. They remain, always ready, always waiting. They know, that if needed, they must rise again to do what can be unpleasant and painful. That is why they are warriors."

"I will do what is necessary."

The words seemed to land on the morning air rich in meaning and portent. Anath shivered slightly despite the warmth of the morning and the room. Something resonated in her and she realized she might be speaking truer words than even she knew. The echo of the words seemed to carry the weight of a solemn vow.

"Then today we begin your new training. No more play! Now comes real work."

As they crossed the practice yards, Anath caught site of the far mountains. They appeared even darker, more ominous, than usual. That they were still deep in shadows despite the lateness of the hour seemed to suggest their darkness was unnatural and an omen. Despite the sun she shivered.

"Attend now!" Turga called drawing her attention. "What you learn now can save us but can also save your own life."

Ravens circled the plains leading to the high mountains. The sleek dark birds circled silently. Even at this distance, they seemed to be waiting and listening to the secrets carried on the wind. Something was coming, they said, and it was clear in each slow loop they made above the barren ground.

The days developed a new rhythm after that for Anath, one of practicing, lessons, and work on her father's lands. Harvests came and the granaries filled with fresh grain. Rumors came of raiders hiding in the mountains.

When bandits came to steal she rode off with the other warriors to reclaim that which was theirs. They found starving and desperate people instead of the hardened brigands they expected. They left enough grain to provide food for those who chose to remain in their camps. Others chose to follow the warriors back to the village. When planting time came, Dagon and Malqart had a larger work force than ever before.

She saw Dagon now out surveying the vast new fields. He nodded his head and she was amazed how little the action meant to her. She returned his nod and then turned away to join a group scouting a ravine to lay traps in case of a future attack.

Over the months, she grew stronger, confident, and sun darkened. She looked more and more like her Mother. Sometimes she saw her father gaze at her and she knew he from the faraway look in his eyes he was seeing her mother.

On her next birthing day, he brought her a finely crafted wooden chest and withdrew a medallion with strange markings. It hung from his fingers on a finely braided leather cord.

"When your Mother came out of the desert she carried a lance, an axe, and this around her neck. Beneath her heart, she carried you as well."

He placed the cord around her neck and stepped back to look at her. In all these years, her father had never been willing to talk about her Mother. Never before had he mentioned she was already with child when she came to his house.

Her Mother, the stranger, found wandering in the desert and brought home to Dagon. All she knew about the past had been learned, sometimes in a taunt from Hadad, or on the knee of the old man Hasai.

"She too was beautiful but also so strong and her heart was worthy."

"Tell me about her, Father." Anath invited.

"She...glowed with love for you and your sister. I would have been the happiest man had she looked at me with that light. Her smile would bring joy to any who saw it. She loved Hadad as if he were her own." He smiled at her. "I know you will be all of those things. You are her daughter, after all."

"Did she ever...my father." She could not look at the man. "Who was my father?"

"She would never say. Not even to me would she talk of that." Her father spoke softly shadows of regret in his voice. "She only said he was part of another place and another time now lost to her. She did not want to dwell in the past, she said, because her future held her children."

"Father, where did my Mother's people come from?" Anath asked. "I know she spoke another tongue before she learned ours. I can still hear some of her words in my head at times..."

"I never knew." Dagon lifted the medallion from her breast. "I never knew anything about her."

She looked at the markings etched onto the surface.

"See that one there?" Dagon pointed to one strange shape arching upwards. "A sea trader passed through one time and said he had seen these. They are called dolphins and they live in the seas far to the north."

"What else did he say?"

"Only that he had seen such markings as these before. He refused to say where other than it was somewhere in the great waters. He said it was forbidden."

"She came from the desert, though, so how would a sea trader know any of this?"

"The man said her people, what he thought were her people, their land had been destroyed, and so they wondered."

"How could a whole land be destroyed?"

"He would not say. He said they explored by ships or became mercenaries in a dozen armies."

"She never told you any of these?"

"She said little about her past. Once you were born she dedicated herself to you and then, later, to your sister. What do you remember?"

"She taught me about the goddess. I remember she sang me songs in her tongue. I know she loved me."

Dagon smiled as if her words brought up his own pleasant memories. "Yes, she was happy and when she was angry or vexed she would use her own language. I am afraid I may have vexed her often."

"Did you care for her?" Anath was aghast she had actually dared to ask the man such a question.

"Yes, I did care for her. I often longed for her smiles to be for me but when she looked at me I saw only gratefulness. I never saw the love I would have desired." He admitted. "I cared for her so much that when she died I wanted to do the same. I am afraid I withdrew too much into myself when she died. I ached in losing her and took it out on all of you. For, that I can only ask your forgiveness. I was a poor substitute for her. You know, you remind me so much of her."

"How is that?"

"You have a look about you, especially those eyes! She too was a warrior: strong and noble. She bore scars of old wounds that spoke of great suffering but also of great courage. She had great skill with every weapon. The first time we hunted together, it was as if she was an animal herself. She seemed to read the mind of her prey. She moved instinctively and with great success on every hunt."

"So, I am a warrior like my mother?"

"It did not surprise me when you made that choice. It was in your blood and the decision an instinctive one. She set great store by that medallion."

"Where did she get it?"

"I do not know what it meant to her or where it came from. She carved the box herself and would never tell me anything about its meaning."

Anath ran her hand over the smooth wood as if she was once more touching the face of her mother. She wanted to cry but would not do so until her father left.

"Before she died, though, she made me swear. If you became a warrior, I was to give it to you with her love, and to tell you these words." He paused in concentration. "She made me memorize this part especially and wanted you to as well…"

"What words were they?"

"I remember now. *Hilka, hilka…*"

That night after they had eaten, and the others had drifted off, she sat by the fire light. She took off the medallion and studied the design in the flickering glow of the flames.

Somewhere in the odd markings might be a key to her mother's people. If there was some hidden meaning it was one she could not decipher. The markings were odd and looked like an eye circling a sphere in which something was trapped or caged. *Some hunting talisman,* she thought.

Around the edges were other symbols etched with great skill and precision despite the small size. The dolphin was one she recognized along with some shapes that might have been flowers or some type of trees. If what Dagon said was true, the waving lines might be for the seas, and might represent her mother's homeland.

She had heard people speak of the seas, vast deserts of blue water, on which people traveled in wooden boxes. Try as she might she could never envision such a strange thing.

The wooden chest was equally mysterious and far heavier than its size implied. Turning it over in her hands she examined it closely. There were other carvings as equally strange as those on the medallion. Its weight bothered her. It was too heavy.

Remembering a story from childhood of a chest with hidden secrets she began probing each side. Finally she opened it but, to her disappointment, she could find no secret compartments with jewels. Childish fancy that! Turning it in her hands, though, she noticed one of the symbols seemed different. She held it closer to the light of the fire. Tiny carvings edged the shape. Peering closer she saw it was surrounded by some of the same symbols on the medallion's edge. There was small thin slit in the wood.

Running her fingers over the smooth wood of the chest, she had a sudden idea. She took the medallion and slid an edge into the slit. She heard something click as if a lock had opened. A faint breeze seemed to whisper to her and she pressed down on the markings she had found. A small drawer sprang out just below and she caught her breath in surprise.

Feeling eyes on her she quickly looked around but saw no one. When she knew she was still alone, she reached into the small compartment, and pulled the drawer out. Revealed was a small flask, as small as a date, and made of clay by a fine artisan. A tiny stopper sealed the top and around the flask were some of the same symbols as the box and the medallion.

What is this, Mother? Holding the small treasure she knew it held a large mystery.

"Speak to me Mother. Walk with me in my dreams again." She felt silly speaking to no one but the moon. Still she whispered, "I need you Mother."

Staring into the dark, she touched the medallion, and asked so many questions. The only answer was the crackling of the fire beside her. Out in the desert, something screamed in the night. It was a new sound, one she had never heard before, and despite the heat from the embers, she shivered and pulled her weapons closer.

Chapter 10

"He left without saying anything?" Asherah asked. They stood in the empty room where Hadad had lived since a baby. It was empty of his weapons and all that was left were the mementoes of his childhood. "He could not be bothered to say goodbye to his family? His own wife and children?"

"I do not think he thinks of us in that light anymore." Malqart inserted and without conscious thought, his eyes went to the hanging on the wall. He glanced at the hanging and then turned away. The young boy had made that himself for his older brother. It had been a proud decoration for years. Now, it hung forlornly in the empty room. "It has been too many years since he really thought of us as his family. His family are that lot in the hills. I have fields to plant." Without another word, Malqart turned and left the chamber. As he walked past, so tall and handsome now and she wished the years back to when he was a child. Especially when she saw the hurt etched in his face. He had so admired his brother and, even though he was a father himself now, he had taken Hadad's rejection of them hard.

"Had we been here more, perhaps we could have averted all of this." Asherah said at last.

"We cannot be blamed for his actions." Anath told her. "This is not some hurt of children that can be mended easily. He is a man and controls his own destiny. He knew what was right for him to do as a man, a brother, a husband, and a son."

"It may not be his fault. He may be under the control of that man who leads the bandits." Asherah noted. "There are rumors he uses some type of magic."

"Silly stories. There is no magic in him. He merely finds the fools and puts a ring in their nose."

Hadad rolled over and reached out for the wine goblet. The woman sprawled beside him muttered in her sleep. He did not even remember her name.

For a moment, his mind went to his bride Sanaa. He had married her to satisfy his father. He had endured the last few years when he knew that life was not what he wanted. There was no more need for him to visit her. He cared more for his horse than he did for his wife and children. It had been a mistake to try and return to that life. Let Melqart breed all the brats the old man could want. It had been months since he left and he was free now.

The woman muttered again and he sat up. Not bothering to put on a robe, he moved to the balcony and saw the night was fighting the dawn. Winter was coming early and though it was always dark in these mountains, it was particularly dismal this morning despite the meager lightening of the eastern sky. Long rolls of fog obscured the hillsides as they crept slowly along amid the rocks and trees.

For months, he had been in a fog. Restless, he had been eager to escape the tight reins of his father's control. He had been weary of trying to curry the old man's favor. Then trying to please a cow faced wife and noisy children.   He had fled to the outskirts and to the camps dotting the western slopes of the mountains.

There he had met the man Mot again. He had worshipped at the altar of blood on the mountain top. Mot had ridden off, and for a moment, Hadad had wanted to follow after him. Instead, he had traveled with a lesser band of Mot's followers as they raided exotic places. At night he heard strange tales and new ideas. He found kindred spirits in these blood stained men.

Now, after months making short raids he was growing restless again. Women, fights, and more sore heads from cheap wine than he cared to remember were no longer enough for him. He needed something more in his life. Yet, nothing here seemed to satisfy him. He needed more in his life than merely lolling about and chasing women.

He remembered Mot talking about his God. It had sounded crazy at the time but now it seemed to make some sense. That deity was a sinister Deity who gloried in death, who encouraged devastation, and commanded the sacrifice of peace in order to forge a new world.

To be part of such a work would bring adventure and glory enough to last a lifetime. Mot understood the gnawing hunger within him because it mirrored his own.

Rising to dress, he made his decision, and he rode away from the raiders camp that morning without a backward glance. He had chosen to seek a life able to satisfy his needs and forever erase his empty and pointless life. It was the darkest mountains, cool and mysterious, that called to him. There he would find Mot. There he would find purpose.

Mot sensed the man had made his decision. The ashes had foretold that he would and now he could see it in his mind. He was sinewy with thick muscles. His long black hair was tied with leather at the back of his head. Sun darkened his skin was the color of an olive tree. His mouth an unsmiling slash across his stony face as he turned toward the center of camp.

Dark stains smeared the space before the pillar set there as an altar and revealed many months of offerings of blood. His people had erected it to honor this new gods of chaos, death and purpose. For a moment, dazzling memories of throbbing drums and screaming voices in a fiery haze consumed him with deep hunger.

Mot strode to the pillar and fell to his knees. Thrusting his fists above his head he gave thanks for his return from this most recent raid. His sword, bloodied and black, he gently laid before the pillar of sacrifice.

The camp was in the higher elevations of the mountains, where the trees straggled to a stop and the snows took over. For months, they had been moving over the mountains from their now barren lands drawing the wolves to them. The human wolves who sought the meat of the hunt and the chaos of death. Now, they paused on the brink of something undreamed of before Mot's words swayed them. Just beyond the far horizon, unseen except in the greedy imaginations of the men, were the warm shores of the seas and their rich trade goods. Under these craggy peaks, his men paused in the cold, and waited for move that would earn them glory.

Raids over the mountains gave them fine cloth as soft and smooth as skin, oils thick and fragrant, and most importantly, fine strong weapons. A few warriors collected jewelry from the corpses for a lover but most simply left them to rot in the sun.

He inhaled deeply the tangy scent of the blood, reliving the thick flowing offering. In his mind, he relived a thousand attacks. Blood, and blood alone, fed the gods of chaos. He was their instrument to appease their eternal hunger.

The droning began in his head until he felt his skull would burst. His eyes filled with swirling colors and he tensed his muscles to withstand the glorious onslaught of sensation from his god. Through heavy lidded eyes he saw the dark swathe of shadows wrapping around his body. It slid around his form in the slow sinuous motion of a serpent. Where it touched his skin, it both burned and froze his flesh. He exalted in the myriad shards of awareness the sensation brought. That shadow was a dark and sinister vine; its hefty fruit produced a bloody cup he gladly drank to the dregs.

Since childhood, he had known he had a special destiny. His Mother had carried him but named no father. She spurned any advances but kept to herself until the birth pangs had brought women creeping to her tent to help. For days she had labored to give him life, blood had flowed like water from her body, and then she could struggle no more.

In desperation, the women had ripped him from the belly of his dead mother even as they were certain he too would soon be a corpse. The gods of death had touched him though and he had taken a deep breath instead. He screamed that he had lived! Some had wanted him sacrificed in fear of the death surrounding his birth. Others, though, saw the signs of his birth as answers to their deepest prayers.

His band grew daily as young men from all directions heard the call of the gods on the wind. Eagerly they joined him to bring sacrifices of death and destruction to the fat and contented. To slaughter the cattle in a thousand homes and villages. He promised them bloody glory and they flew to him, like the carrion, eager for the battles. In their wake, they left fallow, barren fields, slaughtered herds and a silence with no one left alive to lift a mourning song.

A large, black bird swept down then to grasp the top of the pillar and then hopped down to perch on his shoulder. As he finished his prayers and rose, its shrill cry echoed through the camp.

As if summoned, his men appeared from every direction. They were slipping on weapons or hurrying to get the horses. The fowl sailed past as Mot joined them and darted out ahead of them. As one being, they turned their eyes to the south where the bird darted nosily. To the south. It was time; a band of the scouts had returned with reports of fresh ripening cornfields and burgeoning storage bins.

He laughed and ran to his horse. Leaping to its back, he raised his sword high. Whirling it around above his head he gave a cry as shrill as the raven.

"To death!" called Mot as he headed down the hillside at a gallop. The cry was taken up by his men as they charged after him.

Chapter 11

Word of the raiders began to drift to the ear of Anath as she made her circuit through the campfires and villages. First, the traders warned of their presence. Then travelers told of the exploits of the marauders on the far side of the mountains. In hushed and fearful tones, they all shared stories of bloody and cruel raids where none survived. Of the few who lived they all told horrid tales of torture and sacrifice to some obscene new god. Some said it was to an ancient and evil one.

The raiders were ghosts, some claimed while others scoffed at the idea. All agreed they evaded all who sought them. Worse, all agreed, they showed no fear. When outnumbered they turned to confront their pursuers. In their terrible battles they painted the ground red.

Even as she shared the fear of the gruesome stories, Anath wondered if her thoughts about her brother were true. Was he with the raiders? They seemed almost too powerful to stop and might soon destroy the entire land. She had a sudden image of her dreams of fields and a hut engulfed in flames. Through the flames she could see Hadad on Cloudrider. He spun around, his face blackened by soot and blood. Then he rode away with a torch still in his hand. The scene faded as if it had never been.

She was no prophet to have visions and told herself it was only a dream. Still, it made her tense. She knew these strange raiders would appeal to her brother's dark and moody side. Dagon would hate knowing he rode with such as those men. That alone would make the idea even more appealing to her brother.

The winter came and settled harshly in the valley as the days grew more dry and chill. Patrols rode guard around the village to ensure the stored grain and the small herd were kept safe from wandering beasts. Each day as the patrols changed they brought more reports of tracks coming closer and closer to the village.

Some were clearly four legged beasts and some the tracks of man. There were whispers of another type of track that seemed to be both man and beast. Spring could not come too soon this year to suit all of them.

After another tale of such strange footprints had come to his ears, Dagon felt old. He recalled the last time he had seen his first son. He had watched the angry young man leave the great hall, leaving his friends awkwardly standing around.

Chapter 12

The growl was a bloodcurdling shriek loud and close enough that her ears ached. Scorching breath belched onto her neck and foul spittle oozed down onto her in huge slimy gobbets. The eyes of the beast had been serpent like but held the look of a man as well. As bizarre as they had been, worse was the sensation she had that there was some dreadful intelligence behind them.

On her pallet bed atop the roof, Anath struggled awake. Sitting up in the dark she took great gulps of air and then she threw off the hot covering. Hoping the cold night air would help clear her mind she rose and tried to shake off the dream. It had been so unbearably real.

"Anath!" Whispered a frightened voice. Coming through the opening to the roof was her sister.

"Asherah." Seeing her sister's pale face, she opened her arms. The younger girl ran into them. Her face was wet with tears.

"It was an awful dream!" She sobbed into her sister's shoulder. "There was so much blood; so much blood and fear."

Remembering her own dream, she urged her sister to tell her about the nightmare. As her sister talked of the dream, the solid knot of fear settled heavy inside her.

"It was just a dream, little one." As she comforted her sister she sensed there was more than mere chance that both would awake from nightmare. The details were too similar to be an accident. Smoothing down the unruly curls, she tried to calm her sister, but her thoughts were worried. For both to have such dreams...

"Mother said the dreams would grow stronger in times of danger." Asherah said, voicing Anath's own fear. "I remembered that recently. I think it came to my mind as a warning."

"Yes," Anath looked away. "I remember that as well."

"I think there is purpose to all of these dreams. The things she told us as children and now; it is part of a warning."

"She may have been trying to prepare us for something." Anath found herself saying what she swore she would not say.

Asherah leaned back and looked into her Anath's face. "You had the dream too, didn't you?"

Anath considered lying to her sister but knew that would dishonor both her mother's memory and her sister. "Yes, I did."

For a few moments, they spoke and they compared their dreams trying to make sense of the unfathomable.

"We are different. You and I. It is because of her. There is some mystery and I fear we may never learn what it all means." Anath said finally.

"You dreamed as a child. I remember hearing you talk about it when I was little." Asherath said. "That must be your gift. I dream but it is often like a dream of a dream. Except for the ones like tonight."

"When I was a small child I remember dreaming," Anath replied after a few minutes. "More when Mother was alive. At other times, it is hard to say with certainty. There were dreams that were ...odd."

How could she describe that glowing corridor she saw so often? The doorways opening into a million nightmares or a place so delightful she felt she never wanted to leave. Her sister did not need to know about fears that sent her racing away as hideous death snapped at her heels. She had jerked awake bathed in sweat too many times to ever rest easy. Her sister did not need to know that. Not yet. Not unless she too began to dream of such a place.

"Who was our mother?" Asherah whispered in frustration. "Who was our mother to have such abilities or to give such a power to us?"

"I don't know. Witch. Wizard. Demon. Spirit. Wise Woman. "Anath said. "Who knows what she was or what she was capable of doing."

"I never understood what she meant when she talked of her home." Asherah added. "Sometimes it seemed she was speaking in riddles."

"I remember pictures in my head." Her sister nodded. "You had those as well?"

"Yes, I would see scenes of impossible blue water, vast harbors and tall buildings glowing golden in the sun."

"Yes, it was like a magical dream. Surely, no place could be that beautiful."

"Perhaps there was such a place once," Anath replied remembering those pictures as well. "Father said she came from someplace far, far away. He said her people had died because their land had disappeared. Only some, like our mother, escaped. The boats brought them to land and they were cast out to wander the world."

Each lost in her own thoughts, they silently watched the stars in the dark sky, until a faint sliver of moon began to rise. Together, they felt safer, and the horror of the dream receded.

"Anath, Hadad is in trouble, isn't he?"

"Yes, he is, "Anath replied remembering the dream. "He is in grave danger. I fear, though, we can no longer help him. He is somehow tied to the dream."

"I can still hear the cries of the children being torn apart by that vile creature. The sounds of the people being killed; those I cannot forget. We could find Hadad and talk to him."

Anath remembered a part of her dream where her brother tried his best to kill his family. Better for her sister to not learn of that horror. Hopefully, she had not dreamed it already.

"No, he is past argument" Somewhere high in the black heavens above a strange bird cried out. It was a harsh cry that sounded eerie in the darkness. "He has made his choice."

The night air suddenly grew icy and the sisters shivered in the dark. Pulling the woolen cloak over them, Anath felt as if a warning bell had been struck. The dream, she knew with certainty, was a glimpse of what would be but she did not know when.

Her sister, still so young and so innocent, fell back to sleep. Anath, thinking about what must be done, remained awake until the dawn lit the sky.

Mot watched as a proud Hadad rode out with the men. The proud and angry son of Dagon had laughed as three of the women covered his face with kisses and pleaded with him to remain.

The man had been part of Mot's camp for months now. He had ridden on raids and taken his treasures like any of the men. Mot recognized the boy's hunger for adventure and the tantalizing pull of the forbidden offered by his camp. In fact, he counted on it. The women, the wine, and sacred plants were only given to those he wished to draw closer and use them in his own plans.

Some of his men were blunt instruments of muscle and force. Others, like Hadad, had the potential to become more in his scheme. Hadad was more and more becoming his.

He would change his name to reflect his rebirth and his new purpose. Yes, Hadad would die and something new and more terrible would emerge from his ashes.

While most tent's in camp boasted soft women of pleasure, casks of wine and a small horde of treasure, Mot's tent held none of those. His was a dark, tidy tent with just a rug, thick covers, and a stand for his weapons. For long hours, he would work with those strengthening his mind and his body.

As night fell, as the camp settled down, he was sat rigidly on his carpet in honor of his God. The Great Death, the Long Night, the Swift Sleep – these were his food and his wine. These were the sleek women of his dreams and from his dreams came the nightmares others endured.

Soon it would be harvest time again among Dagon's people. The beast would be ready and he, with his soldier of thunderstorms, Hadad, would rain down hell upon them all.

A sound, faint like a sighing wind sang somewhere in the distance and it echoed down empty corridors as she spun through spilling colors to finally halt. Anath opened her eyes and knew she was in that special place of dreams.

Every journey brought something new, sometimes it seemed a cave, sometimes a palace and sometimes, something else; so different she could not define it even to herself. It sparkled now around her like the stars in the night sky but with those familiar rivers of colors so lovely and so changing, she could hardly take it all in.

She glanced down at her arms and saw the colors reflected on her flesh. Breathing deeply the air was different too, cold and crisp. Reaching forward she touched one of the rough walls and felt again the harsh rock texture. The cave of doors then.

A glow, like a sudden sunrise, flashed ahead of her and she saw a woman walking out of the white light. The figure looked familiar, and as she realized, she broke into a run.

"Mother!" A hand came up and she halted just feet from the figure. She knew from other times they could not touch here. Anath might see her mother here but could never reach out to hold her close.

As if illuminated from within, her mother's face glowed and smiled gently at her. She never spoke here but somehow Anath always knew what she meant. There had been many long conversations as she learned from her mother in this strange place.

A hand came up holding something in a tight grip. As the glow receded, Anath gasped seeing a sword held in her mother's hands. With a small graceful movement, she flipped it over and presented the handle to Anath.

Take it child...

Anath hesitated looking carefully at the shining metal and the intricate carvings.

Take it child...you will have need of this in days to come. You are the Sword and the sword is You.

Together you will find your destiny.

It is our way Anath.

Take it my child...begin the journey you were born to take.

Anath reached out and carefully slid her hand around the grip and lifted it from her Mother's hands.

The surface was so smooth it reflected her image and caught every tiny beam of light. It glowed as she held it.

It felt right in her hand. It was as if she had been born holding such a weapon. The weapon seemed to call to her as if it had been crafted ages ago for her grip alone. She spun around moving into the well-rehearsed steps of battle. It was light but not weak. Its sleek lines and subtle weight hid great strength. The blade spoke to her somehow and told her that it possessed a purpose.

"Mother, what am I to …" The glowing hallway was empty. The long corridors were empty of anything but herself and the mighty weapon.

She stepped out into the familiar and long practiced moves of parry, slash and thrust. Her muscles rippled hoisting the blade with ease. The weight was so finely balanced that she could handle it like no other weapon she had ever used.

A wind whispered past her weaving its way through the empty corridors of stone. As it passed a voice echoed….*Take the weapon my child; it was destined for you…It is, and has always been, the Sword of Anath.*

Chapter 13

The last of the harvest had been brought in and the people were deep in the enjoyment of a hard task finally completed. The festival was full of dancing and merry making. The storage bins bulged with the grains, piles of corn were cut and waiting for grinding, and the last of the nuts and fruits dried and bagged for the winter. The smoky air filled with the scent of aromas of roasting meat and savory drink.

Children and old men danced joyously around the blazing fire. They leaped and jumps with equal parts abandon and skill. Everywhere in the camp there was laughter as the excitement grew. This was a time of celebration as couples were wed, births celebrated, and romances initiated. Mountains of food rose to be quickly devoured and rivers of wine flowed.

It was also a time of initiation.

Anath and Asherah followed silently the willow like woman leading them up the mountain in the darkness. Anath shivered wishing she had brought a cloak. The night was clear but, from the mountainside, the many fires below turned the landscape into smoky rivers of movement. This far away the music faded to just a throbbing of drums that mimicked the erratic beat of her heart.

Asherah, walking beside her, looked around with wide eyes and seemed ready to bolt. The tension in the young girl made her movements awkward.

"It is alright." Anath leaned down to whisper to her young sister. She gave her shoulder a small squeeze. "You will live."

Anath looked up the hillside toward their destination. They followed the women to a small cave cut into the mountain. As the neared the light of their torches revealed stone steps cut into the opening. A frieze of carvings of animals, trees and fruits ringed the opening as well. Flickering light glowed from deep within.

The legends said once, long ago, their people had hidden in such caves as the world turned to fire and died. Deep in the womb of the earth, they had found food and water to keep them alive while the demons and the devils danced their death battles. Every day the heavens rang with the fury of the confrontations with the raging gods. As a child, that was always the story that sent her hiding under benches or behind strong doors.

As stepped down the steps further into the cave, two elderly women seemed to step right from the rock walls. Slowly they came to the young women and closer it was clear they were ancient women. Hands with skin like gauzy leather reached out to gently grasp their arms. The women lead the way inside, deeper they descended, into the shadowy core of the cave. The torches glowed, hissing and flickering, casting strange dancing shadows on the walls as they passed.

Jars of scented oils, leather bags with spices and strands of drying herbs filled the caverns with their aroma. The smell was so strong it burned the nostrils. So thick was the air it caused Anath to feel lightheaded.

Finally, the cavern opened up into a wider space, and the women set their torches in niches in the walls. On the floor were two pallets. Nearby were plates of fruits, nuts, and bread. A pitcher of wine sat nearby with two small cups.

"Here you will shed your present life."

Two other women, younger than the others, came from the shadows carrying clothing over their arms. Quickly the two girls removed their clothes and pulled on the clean garments. Their clothes, they knew, would be burned in a ritual on the same fire the village people were dancing around.

As the women left with their clothes, two others, a man and a woman, entered carrying arms filled with sheaves of wheat and heavy heads of corn. These they placed along one wall and then they bowed to the two girls before they hurried out. They were eager to return to the festivities.

A drum sounded outside the cave signally that ritual had truly begun. Torches flickered in the corridors. The thrum echoed in the cavern accompanied by the haunting wordless song of the harvest chanters. They sang no words; for how can a human speak the language of the Gods? Then the procession finally entered.

The leader, a woman chosen this year as priestess of the harvest, raised a hand and halted the small group. She was familiar to Anath but she could not recall the woman's name. She lived on the far side of the oasis to the west.

"Blessings of the great Gods! The Gods of the harvest bestows their blessings." She scanned the wealth of items stacked throughout the cave. Then, as if satisfied, she raised her hands and turned to each direction and then bowed to the fire. "The people accept the blessing of the harvest and give sacrifice in return."

The others who had followed the woman now came forward put of the shadows. Carrying bowls, platters, jewelry, bundles of fine cloth, and more wine they placed them around the chamber.

"The Gods of the harvest bestows bounty." Anath recited the words as she had been taught.

The priestess bowed again and gave her reply: "The people accept the blessings and give in return." Anath received the words she had heard since childhood. A memory bubbled to the surface of her mind. As a very small child, before her mother died, she had heard that phrase and had seen a tear fall down her strong mother's cheek. Childlike, she had kissed it away and her mother had held her tightly, her face buried in her childish curls. "Why do you cry?" she had asked. Her Mother had given her another tight hug as she whispered, "Because I am so blessed....you are my bounty."

As if the memory was a catalyst, *something* unlocked inside of her. Where moments before she had been almost bored by the ritual she was not intensely alert. Frowning she looked around. Everything nearby was normal. Too long a hunter, trained in all the hunter skills of observation, she trusted her senses and so her eyes searched the chamber.

Cautiously she peered around, seeking whatever it was that had so suddenly heightened her senses. Past the group, she had almost missed it completely as it hid deep in the shadows of the tunnel. As she watched the dark changed. There, something shifted within the blackness of the shadows. It moved in an odd bulky manner and so hard to see that she might, almost, have imagined the movement.

There was a sense of menace and a certainty that something evil brooded there in the dark. Fear froze her heart in her breast. A vision of Mot speared her mind with sickening clarity. The darkness perfectly matched his cruelty and she could believe he or some demon stood poised and hulking in the black depths of the corridor. His bloodthirsty ways were vile enough to spawn such an evil presence.

She looked again and the dark shadow remained hidden amid the darkest of the gloom. Whatever it was it grew heavy and thick as the rest of the ritual finished.

She cast her mind back to her lessons and was vexed realizing how little she had paid attention. Not like her sister; that was a strength of Asherah. Listening to the priests drone on about spells, protections, and battling a spirit world she could not see had not captured her attention. Not the way the practice field had. Now, she desperately wished she had listened closer during those lessons.

Had he cast some evil charm to travel in shadows? Was he really here or was it a mere illusion sent to trick them? Was her imagination and the aromas filling the closed cave playing with thoughts?

No, there was something there and she knew its source was Mot. Why else would she suddenly think of him? It was not the aroma of the spices or the flicking light of the torches making her feel lightheaded. She shivered again despite the almost suffocating heat in the lighted chamber.

As if to confirm her earlier feelings, a wintry draft snaked through the cave, and slithered past the feet of the priestess. Had he somehow made himself vapor to spy on the sacred rights? No; this was something different more of a threat than even Mot and his army.

Beyond the shadows, she knew that something more, something worse, lurked in the darkness of the tunnel. She had the feeling that it merely waited its time. She feared when it finally appeared it would take the form of something malevolent and ominous. Something that would be invisible to her until too late.

The cave shuddered all around her, it shimmered slightly, the people becoming momentary blurs before settling back into their normal shapes. She looked at the others, and at Asherah, but they had apparently not experienced anything out of the ordinary.

Without looking she sense something stood there in the opening. It was so dark it was like shadow yet strangely it conveyed an impression of solidity and form. Like a wicked child, it was peering at the ceremony, and was mocking the life and joy the ritual represented.

Images, flashes of things only seen in her nightmares, flickered through her head. She knew this thing. Its sharp claws and foul spittle filled her dreams. She had felt its hot breath burning her flesh. Suddenly, her heart was thudding in her chest. It was a thing of such evil it could make bones turn to water.

Like a thirsty beast it licked it lips and stood poised in the dark ready to pounce. It would, without a thought or compassion, strike with deadly accuracy. Its fearful strength would drain the life from everyone there.

She wanted her new sword but knew it was useless against this thing of smoke and shadow.

"Let the water and the wine mix to bring new life and prosperity." Anath dragged her attention back to the ritual as the oldest woman spoke. With her words she held high a bowl of new wine.

She drank from the bowl and then passed it to the woman next to her. Each woman drank deeply, and solemnly, as she took her turn.

Putting her worry aside, Anath focused on the movements of the ritual. Asherah now took the bowl from the old woman and carefully, to not spill a drop, she took a long sip. The last to receive the cup was Anath.

The others had told her that if the group was in a playful mood, or if a person was one who was considered too serious, they might leave the bowl nearly full. The person targeted would wake with a sore head the next morning and many jokes from friends.

The bowl was nearly empty, Anath was happy to see. There was enough left, however, to reveal one of the women thought she needed to enjoy life more. She nodded, accepting the advice, and then drained the bowl dry. With a bit of bravado she set it down, wiping her mouth with the back of her hand as she had seen the warriors do. *Face the correction with courage*. It was a wisdom she had heard them say to one another on the fields. What was good enough for them was also good enough for her.

Anath felt the wine course through her veins and sensed it already making her a little lightheaded. Trying to focus her vision she saw the shadowy form still crouching at the opening. She could only stare. *Is it real or merely the wine*? She had little time to think before the others turned her attention to other matters.

Several of the women looked at each other and gave the blessing as required. Then they all jumped to their feet with a cry and in response the drumming began. It grew livelier and intense as the procession circled the cavern and then hurried out. They hurried through the corridors holding their torches aloft. Their cries rang through the night as they rushed to join the revelry down the mountain.

The feeling of eyes watching her had evaporated as quickly as it had come. Standing at the entrance to the sacred cave, she waved a smiling response to the comments of the well-wishers. Breathing heavily she forced herself to dispel the thoughts which had attacked her. Asherah quickly hurried back into the cave. She was eager for the great adventure of the night.

Each harvest, two people would be selected by lot to sleep with the Gods in the mountain. It did not matter if they were men or women. They represented the fruitfulness of the present harvest and the promise of the future one.

They would spend the night here, eating the food and drinking the wine. All the food, the bundles of finely woven cloth, and jewelry would be theirs to keep in honor of their fulfillment of their duty to the Gods. She smiled as she saw Asherah fingering the trinkets and danced around with a length of grass green cloth held to her.

"Come!" Her sister called to her as she danced.

Anath groaned, but allowed herself to be yanked to her feet by her sister, but gave in to the lighthearted play.

"Look at this!" Asherah held high a fine medallion made of tiny clay beads and pieces of stones with the glint of gold. The bags of food represented the sacrifice of her people to show their appreciation to the gods. To insure the timely rains and the gentle winds each family had done their part. In other harvests, she had packed up such gifts and offerings and left them in this cave.

Next year, it would be time for Asherah to be in charge of the clan's gifts. The settlement survived because everyone had a role to play and no matter how minor the role it was needed.

It reminded her that she had a role to play this night. She settled down on the rugs. *Now,* she grimaced, *if I can just remember all of it...*

"Once, the world was all dark and without any sky, moon, or sun."

"All were blind, hungry, and like wild animals in the night…" Her sister replied with an impish gleam in her eyes.

Giggling at times, feeling strange reciting the formal words, they at last finished the ritual.

Asherah settled down beside her, plopped a huge grape in her mouth, and readied herself to listen. "As the eldest you must repeat the stories. All the legends and the histories; everything! *As storyteller you are teacher, priest, and parent.*" Her sister repeated the lines of the ritual as she plopped a date in her mouth. "I will eat and grow fat on this feast."

Anath pushed the meat platter toward her sister and moved the sweets away.

"You will become too fat to lift a spear or shoot an arrow. You will be unable to run in the hunt. Be careful or you will be unable to bend over to put on your own sandals!"

As Anath finished, her sister made a face but also grinned. Anath remembered sitting at the fires and listening to the stories as a child. Taking a deep breath she began the traditional opening to the first story.

"These are the stories of our people as they have been taught, as they have been learned…"

Even as she shared the stories, as the ritual required, Anath felt the pull of the shadowed portal leading back outside.

She could not shake the feeling that something cold and soulless had peered around the people who had come to bless the ones chosen to be with the Gods this night.

Nor, could she shake the feeling that once more something had - shifted - this night, forever changing the world she knew.

Chapter 14

Blood painted the face of a child's doll a dull red. Asherah could not seem to take her eyes from that one small detail. Dragging in a ragged breath she turned away unable to bear the sight of the remains of the family scattered around the hovel's meager campfire. The charred remains of the fire lay as cold and dead as the bodies around it.

All the others in the party were just as silent. They had all seen death before in many of its guises but they had never seen bodies…shredded…in this vicious way. It was as if some vicious animal had…

"Asherah!" Anath, followed by several warriors trotted into the encampment. As they took in the bewildering scene, Asherah saw a new and unusual worry etched on all their faces. Her sister spoke at last: "We saw the smoke and came as quickly as we could. What happened?"

"We don't know. We were gathering some cattle and saw the smoke and hurried to help. We thought that their hut had caught fire." Asherah spoke in a hoarse whisper. "When we arrived, well, this was what we found."

"We scouted around looking for anything that would explain this slaughter. We found the tracks of *something*." Spoke one of the men standing to one side. He pointed to the ground rimming the camp. Keena was a great hunter as well as a warrior. Despite his advanced years he was a formable fighter. "Very strange tracks. They are like nothing any of us have ever seen before."

The warriors walked to where he had gestured. Crouching, she Anath saw the imprint left by something massive.

"We caught its trail as we came back from the ridges. At first, we thought it was just a very large sand cat searching for water." An almost human shaped hand but of much larger size.

She placed her hand in its print and was amazed at the depth and size. There were also the clear marks of large, sharp talons. "Instead, they led here.

"We did not see it," Keena said. "We found only what it had done. I have not seen such a sight before."

Anath turned, frowning, to view the scene of death. A sudden fleeting image of massive jaws and dripping teeth seen in a dream came to her. One of the monsters locked behind those bizarre dream doors. Why think of one of those now? Simple, the size and the ferocity of its attack were new in her experience. Then, to hear the oldest hunters admit the same thing was chilling.

She wondered if her face was as drained of color as Asherah's face was and hoped not.

"Come, walk with me sister." Asherah said. She glanced at the other warriors as she led her sister a little distance away. Asherah walked away from the scene as the warriors set off to begin the funeral preparations. She led them to the far edge of the camp before she spoke. "Anath, we searched but we could find no survivors."

"Then, we must go help see to their graves now."

"Wait. Riders came earlier, just after we arrived, and said that other smoke had been seen in the hills. They fear all of this is Mot's doing. They call him an evil priest. Anath, if he works in some dark magic you *must* be careful."

Those were worrisome words, especially coupled with what she had been told earlier.

"Asherah, Keena says he has never seen such tracks before."

"If Keena does not recognize them -." She did not have to complete the sentence, both knew its full meaning.

"It is too late to start after whatever made them. We'll have to camp here."

"We must tend to the family, Anath. Then set guards."

Hours later, the sky was growing dark as the flames shot higher into the sky. The duties outlined how the dead were to be honored and though, sometimes the rules of conduct were heavy, now she could see they helped in such times. Going through the motions and the rituals for the death farewell meant you did not have to think for a while and she could push the grief aside. For a time at least, for a little while, but then they were finished and the pain returned.

As the twilight wind fanned the flames consuming the bodies, Asherah wiped away her tears and knew she was not alone. Nearly every face around the fire bore the tracks of tears for those lost.

Across the sands, a sound echoed causing them all to halt and feel a weakness in their bones. It was a piercing howl, bizarre and foreign, echoing from the far mountain range. The sound swirled around them before it faded leaving a dark and silent night.

The lack of sound was so odd. Asherah instinctively reached for her bow. Anath clutched the hilt of her sword tighter. She noted the others, even the most seasoned of them, bringing their own weapons closer at hand in this suddenly strange night.

"We will take turns standing guard tonight." Anath told the others as she took out her sword and settled against one of the rocks. "I will take the first watch."

At dawn, after an uneasy night, the group returned to the village. Anath met with the leaders and answered their questions. Her father held her back as they filed out of the courtyard. "Anath, Asherah tells me of a monster, is this true?"

"I do not what it was. There was something. It left a track none of us had ever seen."

"There were traders who came through while you were gone. There is talk that Mot uses spells and arcane incantations to raise some demon. It may be nothing but travelers' tales, but when I heard of the beast you tracked, it made me pause."

"Father, the night of the harvest ritual, just as the women left us in the cave, I thought I saw something."

"This beast you saw it there in the caves? What did you see?" Her father asked.

"Shadows, mere shadows, but I felt as if something was there and it watched us."

"Warriors?"

"No. It was like smoke but it moved like a man or a beast like a man." She admitted. He might not believe her but it was what she had seen. "It felt...evil."

Her father frowned off into the distance. "The medallion...there was a thing your Mother did before she slept sometimes. I asked and she said it helped her dream with purpose. She did not tell me much but, perhaps, daughter, even that small piece of knowledge will help you. It may be the folly of an old man but I think that it will be important for you to know. Let me tell you what she said."

Anath halted, and there in the hallway, she listened intently to all that her father told her. Later, as he walked away she turned toward her own bed with her thoughts in confusion. *There is so much I do not know*, she thought in vexation.

She worried her lack of comprehension might lead to disaster.

Chapter 15

In the dark night soft cold winds breathed across silken sands lifting clouds of dreams to dance into the stars. Clasping the talisman from her mother's box, she finished the phrases her father had taught her and felt drowsy. Eyelids falling closed Anath fell into sleep and opened her eyes to find she was in a familiar long corridor.

All around her were the peculiar stones she had come to know from her dreams. The walls shone with the same lustrous glow with from the veins of shining color. She had followed the directions given by her father and now was in this place.

As always there was a strange quality to this particular dream. She recognized the place from earlier dreams but now there was so much more detail. Although she could not have explained what she meant the place felt less dreamlike and more real.

"Anath." Turning, she saw Asherah coming toward her. Her sister's face as confused as she knew she must have on her own.

"Where are we, Anath? How did we get here?" her sister asked. "Is this place even real? I was asleep in the school."

"What is happening?" Anath repeated softly. Quickly she told her sister of her father's advice. "It must have helped because it is all more substantial than it had been earlier. Plus, you are here."

"Yes, it seems so real. Exotic but real. Have you been here before?"

"I have walked halls like this. This place looks familiar to those in my earlier dreams."

"Anath! I have been here before!" Asherah's face beamed. "So have you. When we were little."

Anath gazed around in sudden recognition. "Yes, yes it does. It looks like the place where Mother -."

"The place she showed us when we were children." Anath tried to catch all the details of the halls at once. "The banners on the walls. Look at how they glow as if molten silver flowed through every stitch. See, there are even the symbols from the box!"

"Look! The large fish leaping out the water! A dolphin; the trader said that symbol was called a dolphin. Until I saw that on the box, Anath, I thought that was just part of a dream I had as a child."

"Our mother had many special gifts. I am learning more every day it seems." Anath said. "One of those skills was this. I do know what she called it but it apparently some type of dream traveling."

"Is that what this place is?" Asherah asked eagerly looking around trying to peer through windows and doors. "A place out of our dreams? Is so, she should be here because I have so longed to be with her. Is she here? Mother!"

"Asherah! Wait, stay here, it is not exactly the same. This is our memory I fear. It is almost the same but there are differences. Only the things I remember are here so it cannot be the same. This may be dangerous."

Her sister froze in place and turned back cautiously. Asherah took a deep breath fighting down the sudden disappointment. Anath was right though, and reluctantly she followed her sister's gaze.

"I know little one. I would like to walk with her one more time as well." She patted her sister's shoulder. She had been very young the last time mother had walked with them in their dreams down the shining halls.

"Father told me of something she would do to find purpose in her dreams and I tried it myself."

"Then how did I come to be here as well?" Her sister mused. "I do not know exactly what happened or how I came to find myself here."

"Somehow, perhaps of who our mother was or some other reason, we are connected. It has been that way since we were children."

"Maybe the dream walks with our mother helped forge a special bond." Asherah suggested.

"Possibly. Maybe it is because we are her daughters. I do not know."

Anath frowned as she focused on their surroundings. She saw she had been right when she had said there were many differences. While overall there was the sense it was more substantial and real it still lacked. There was not the detail of the earlier visit as a child. There was a hazy aspect to many details, like a footprint smudge in the sand. There was something there but just what she could not say with certainty. She walked to a wall and saw her hand disappear into it past the wrist. Jerking it out, she stepped closer to her sister. She glanced down at where she and her sister stood and realized it seemed substantial enough but the further and deeper she looked the more obscure were many of the details. Was there some additional skills involved in accessing this dreamlike world? *There is so much I do not know!*

"When we were here before," Anath spoke at last. "We were here because of mother."

"Yes, she called us here to speak with us and teach us."

"What were you doing today?" Anath asked suddenly as an idea came to her.

"I was hunting near the water pool."

"You fell near a cliff, didn't you?"

"Yes, I slipped and nearly -," She paused. "How did you know?"

"I think I understand, maybe just a little, about how we are here." Anath relied.

"Sister, you must share more of our mother's gifts than we knew. You knew I was in trouble today and you called us to this place."

"Asherah, how do you know it was not you?"

"Once, when you were a small child, mother was walking with me telling me about something in her past."

"As she did often with me. Surely, that was not so strange a thing for her to do."

"She suddenly raised her head, as if she heard something I did not. She dashed back to the house." Anath told her. "I arrived in time to see you crying on the floor where you had fallen. She scooped you up with such a look of concern on her face."

"She heard me cry out!" Asherah laughed. "Hardly any special talent."

"No, we were too far away for that." Her sister told her. "*You* did it, Asherah. Somehow, you called her to you and she came to you in the flesh. Just as we have both come to this place in our dreams. You."

Asherah turned away to look closer at their surroundings. It was clear she was struggling to make sense of what was being suggested.

"This is different because it is not all our mother's creation." Anath told her. "It is also your creation. I remember things that are not here" Anath told her. "The difference is in you!"

"No, there is no way. Such a thing is impossible."

"Like this place of dreams?" Anath pressed her. "It is still rough and perhaps lacks the strength of her abilities but you will learn. Clearly, this is a talent you have from her. It is in you to learn."

Her sister listened closely but then walked to her, closed her eyes, and touched her face. The contact sent a shiver through Anath. The hallway around them rippled and then settled back into its previous form. No, thought Anath, not the same. The hallway seemed even more real – somehow.

"What did you do?" She asked Asherah in confusion.

"Something just told me to find your memories and this place would be more real." She looked around and smiled. "It seemed to work."

Grinning, Anath had to agree. "Your talent and my memory, huh?"

"It is not me, Anath. This is an echo of a real place. I envisioned a warm tent in the desert but we came back to this place. It is clearer, but it is not my creation. Somehow, maybe somewhere, this place is real. Maybe it is a place from our mother's life in her forgotten land."

"I had never thought of that. It would make sense she would create a place she knew well."

"There is still so much we do not know. So little time to master it all to keep us safe from Mot."

Asherah moved closer to her sister as she finished speaking and they sank to the glistening floor of this dream world. A small glowing fire appeared beside them and the younger girl grinned again.

"Maybe you are right about me having some talent. I was chilled. Now, tell me more Anath. Tell me everything you remember or know about her. It is time we stopped wondering around like children. If we are right and we have this legacy from our mother, we must grasp it as a tool."

Suddenly in her hands Anath held the gleaming sword. She caught her sister's eye: "Perhaps we should start with this."

Chapter 16

The seasons came and their lives fell into the common and pleasant patterns they had enjoyed before Hadad had left them. Melqart had nearly replaced Dagon in the duties on the village council. He had taken over most of the daily functions of the farm and the trading.

The torches flickered with myriad colors bright against the night sky. Music and laughter filled the air as Oreb and Shebal celebrated the birth of a new child and the end of a bountiful harvest.

After the hard work of recent days, everyone was ready for some relaxation. The new storage bins were filled with fresh corn and wheat. The herds were larger than in many years. The trading had been good with fewer raids than some seasons.

That worried some, mainly because of the stories of an army massing in the mountains under some marauder's banner. Other, laughed off such tales as empty fears. The stories persisted though. Whispers came of charred lands and prisoners sacrificed to a god of death, but those shadows were far from everyone's thoughts tonight.

Tonight was for joy, dancing, and flirting. Anath leaned against the baskets holding fragrant fruits, far enough to enjoy the cool air of the night, yet near enough to be warmed by both the music and the laughter.

She was tired, but happy, she realized. These were her people and this was her home. She could not imagine ever leaving this place.

For once, Asherah was the serious one. Anath could see her in deep conversation with the priests. She had so many questions. The more they learned and traveled in that dream world, the more questions she had. Anath was tired of work. She wanted to enjoy the end of this harvest and festivities.

One of the young men, caught her eyes through the dancing flames of the fire. Everything she needed or wanted was right here. Yes, it was time for more pleasant activities. She caught the young man's eyes and smiled. Yes, she was very happy.

Chapter 17

As the harvest came and the first chill fingers of cold touched the nights, the stories of the raiders increased. More people wandered into the village seeking to escape the attacks. Life went on but everyone was fearful with the new reports of more raids and deaths

Asherah tossed the roll of cloth so it spilled like wine across the tiles of the courtyard. Despite herself, Anath found her eyes tantalized by the play of light over the fine weaving. The past months had been pleasant one with many benefits. Not only had a caravan of traders made their way past the mercenaries of Mot, they had carried rare treasures such as the finely woven material the women were gloating over all through the village.

Anath fingered the warm red cloth in spite of herself; it was soft and glided through her fingers like cool water. The rich, warm color was the same deep glow of the firestones the traders sometimes carried.

"See, it will be a most lovely gown!" Her sister proclaimed as she rolled it back around the holding staff. "Or, a mantle perhaps to keep out the night's chill."

"I am sure whatever you select it will be very nice."

"It is your material though! You should make some decision. It is too lovely to let go to waste."

"It was a gift and I had no wish to offend." She glanced down at the tunic that fell to her knees, held in place by the leather belt and the tall-laced leather sandals she was wearing. Hers was the garb of the warrior and though the rich color of the cloth gave her pause, she knew it was not for her. "I do not see myself in such finery."

"Warrior or not, you are still a person Anath. You do not have to forgo the more pleasant rewards of life."

She looked at her sister pointedly and changed the subject. "The scouts are coming back today. I must hear their reports. There is still the threat of the raiders. I am anxious to hear what they learned of Mot and his men."

"I want to forget about him! I want it to be the way it was when we were children." Although she was older, there was still much of the child in her sister.

"I know...Childhood is over, though." Anath spoke softly as she watched her sister sink to the bench. Her face sobered and suddenly she was looking very sad. All around them, their once familiar life was shifting like the sands in the deep desert and sometimes it seemed they would lose their way.

Seeing the look on her sister's face, she tried to lighten the mood. "Well, I will not like it, but you can arrange for something to me made of the cloth. Perhaps if you make me something along the lines of what I am wearing, I might find an excuse to wear it occasionally. No promises, and just for you, my sister."

"Oh, Anath! I know it will be lovely. Do you want it the same length or shall I make it longer?"

"You may decide what form the cloth will take. I will wear it, whatever it may be."

Shaking her head at the other woman's reluctance to wear fine clothes, Asherah, turned to leave. At the door she paused: "Even warriors sometimes wear finery. Remember that my sister."

The training in the bow was proceeding well. Old Turga, sitting in the opening to the tent, watched in approval as Anath and the other warriors worked groups of the women, children and youth. They had accelerated the training with the defection of Hadad and some of his worthless friends. Now, even the youngest of them was learning to fight.

Glancing up, the old man saw the sinuous cloud of dust crawling down the mountainside. That much smoke meant many horses and many men. He rose to shout, but before he could, one of the warriors had seen it as well and sounded the alarm. Turga turned back into the tent and prepared as best he could to assign the weapons as the anxious children, youth, and warriors hurried to him.

Mot rode behind the beast, glorifying in the connection to the creature, as loped down the mountainside. He could feel it just as the priest has said he would. Their hearts beat as one and every breath was one they shared.

In this form, it was a foul thing smelling of blood and butchered meat. It was a strange misshapen thing as well. A monster – not all man but not all animal – a beast of matted fur, bulging muscles and dreadful voracious temper.

It ranged ahead of him clearing a path. The bestial face was a terrible thing to behold. The sight of it, snarling and sniffing the air with a snout, was enough to turn bones to jelly and make endless nightmares a reality.

They had followed in its wake as the creature ripped apart armies and rampaged through settlements. Its visage, roaring with bared teeth, dripping spittle, bits of flesh hanging from its mouth and dank with blood, was enough to cause hearts to seize in the chest of even the stoutest raider. The men, hardy fighters everyone, held back in the face of the creature.

Good, Mot thought, they fear both it and me in equal measure. We are one!

He could feel the animal.

He could see through its eyes.

He could taste its desire for blood.

A hoarse scream split the air and the men halted and Mot continued on to see as the roars and shrieks mingled. He suddenly tasted the spurting hot blood in his mouth. He felt the deep bite of fangs into flesh and knew the feel of chomping gory slabs of meat.

As he rode closer he saw that one weary raider had stepped too close to the snarling beast. The spray of blood painted a wide cluster of raiders. The air echoed with the terrible gurgling screams. They had tumbled over themselves stepping away to leave their cohort to his grisly fate.

"Cowards!" Mot grated as he rode by, close enough to see into the eyes of the door man's head tossed aside as the beast fed. The shaggy haired creature paused, lifting man-like eyes to glare at him as he passed. Mot stared by and rode on ahead knowing the creature and he were linked. A low growl rolled up from the depths of the beast but Mot did not look away.

"We are safe my brave ones." He spoke as he moved his horse forward. "The thing could not get away. You saw the ritual; the creature is mine to command. With him I will conquer!"

Torn by memories of their terror and their pride, the men followed in fear. One bile rising horror after another had them nearly gibbering like infants since they left camp. More than one felt a looseness in his bowels just seeing the creature. Yet, they had to go one; they had seen a shadow rise at the power of the incantations and settle on Mot like a cloak. The longer he and the beast were in tandem, though, the more strangely he acted. They needed to battle flesh and blood. To drive off their fears.

Mot, seeing the village of Dagon ahead, already bursting into flames from the first assault, stood up with a look of ecstasy on his face, and he screamed an order to the beast. "Attack! Storytellers through the ages will sing the glories of this harvest feast! Release!"

The men struggling to hold the beast by long chains abruptly fell back. The creature e off the collar and lunged forward with a howling bellow. The cry echoed with brutal force through the night.

The bravest of the fighters hesitated but then, like dark birds of death Mot and his men rushed after the thing with swords high. Mot cried out, "Hail, him! See the mighty God of death!"

"Hail, him! See the God of death!"

Anath clutched her side as she trotted into the shadows between two buildings and crept up the narrow, hidden passageway. The wound in her side was agony.

"Hail, him! See the God of death!" The call echoed through the streets from nearly all sides. It almost drowned out the cries of the dying and those scattering in fear.

Burning with every breath, and, despite the wad of cloth she had tied to her waist, she could feel the warm blood flowing through her fingers. There was so much blood...

She wanted nothing so much as to simply lie down and give into the pain. Maybe in that oblivion the images in her head would leave her. Those horrid cries of people torn to pieces by that creature. The shrill howls of torment and agony.

Friends of childhood and students she worked with daily all dead. Hot tears coursed down her face but she ignored them. More important than their losses, her aching grief, was the threat to her own life.

She had an obligation to her people; the duties spelled it out in the laws of revenge and justice. She must live to make them pay for this sacrilege.

The first band of mercenaries who had taken her city had swept in under the guise of travelers. Then they turned on them all to destroy. They had abused the ancient laws of hospitality her people treasured.

There were people who knew she still lived and was on the run through these dark streets. She would find help but would it be before she was found by the savages? They would hunt her down and kill her without mercy.

"Hail, him! See the God of death!"

She peered through the orange flames blazing all around to get her bearing. Blocking out the cries of shock she tried to think. So much destroyed; so much left to be done if they wished to survive the night. Survive she would. She would also teach them to fear that they had not killed her. By the grace of the goddess, she would teach them that lesson well.

At a sudden cry she froze and pushed herself deeper into the ebony shadows. Men swept past where she hid and in the light from the torches they carried she could see them clearly. .Her suspicions had been right. In the flickering lights she saw the markings on their skin. Those markings had been drawn for her by survivors of some of the distant raids. Sinuous shapes crawling up arms and across their faces. Etched with knives and filled with soot they reflected the foul worship of Mot. Some of Yamm's men had borne those markings as well.

Even then had he been aligned with Mot? Had her brother known? Yamm, Mot and Hadad. Suddenly it all seemed to make sense that Mot would ensnare Yamm in his schemes. If Yamm could be won over it would have been an easy thing to seek out her brother as well.

Mot had doomed himself with the actions here. There was no corner of hell itself where he could hide to keep safe. The ancient laws were sacred: hospitality, protection, and water were to be given freely and without fear. The duties were clear about the punishment for such disregard of the ancient laws. To lose both kindness and honor was to become a beast.

They strangers had turned on them quickly and brought up weapons. Others had slipped in to surround them as well.

"You are a long way from home," Anath had said to the one who seemed to lead the men. "I did not know that the customs of people of Mount Cassius were so different from ours. We share, after all, so much in common. I know that both your stories and songs also recall a common source within the Ancient of Days."

The man laughed. "The heart of the people is on Mount Cassius and there is the true god! You are weak!" Mot's man spat into the puddle of water on the ground. "The day has come and we raise the cry of the god of thunder! The spears you parade so proudly will be broken like stacks of rotten sticks"!

Then, the others of his band had ridden in, and the world had exploded in fire and fear.

Someone should have killed him the day he had marched into the region, she thought slumping down into the shadows adjusting the makeshift bandage. *The very day he first walked he should have been wiped away like something foul on the bottom of a sandal.* She had to focus, too many emotions whirled in her head. *No, when he first took breath!*

So much would have been spared. So many lives would still live if only things had been different; if she had been different. Well, if she lived, she would have learned her lesson. She would carry the scars of it for years. If the goddess granted her life this night. Outnumbered, and probably still surrounded by Mot's men, she had no weapons and could only hide.

When only silence rode on the wind, she started back up the crooked little alleyway, climbing into the hillside and the caves she knew where hidden here. Several of the merchants, the winemakers and the cheese sellers, liked to store their products in the cool of the smaller caves. With a little luck, she could climb to the other side of the hill before they even realized the caves existed.

Kept there as well were the healing salves and potions the priestesses used for injuries. She had helped carry a load of them only a few months earlier.

The maw of the cave was dark and silent. Moving sure-footedly into the dark opening, she reached for the wall, and found the rope kept there to guide a person when they visited the caves. She clung to the rope and hurried into the darkness. Finally, she turned into an alcove. It was filled with jars and baskets and a heady mix of aromas.

She felt along the wall and found the lamp. After several tries with flint the wick flamed to a sullen brightness. It seemed to begrudge even that tiny flame. Dropping in exhaustion, she lifted one of leather pouches into her lap. It was difficult; her hands were shaking from the effort of the climb. From one of the bundles she pulled out plants, herbs and salves.

Pulling a clay pot closer she slowly she mixed in oils and slowly spread them on to small rags she could use as bandages. Even that small effort had her heard spinning but she forced herself to move.

Taking a deep breath, she braced herself and tore away the sodden bandage from the gaping wound gasping as fresh dizziness washed over her. She struggled to ride the agony. Her vision blurred again as she worked and once she had to pause for her sight to return to normal. She had done this dozens of times for others. Why was it so hard now? She wiped away the globules of drying blood grunting in pain. She placed the fresh salve on and gasped as a fresh fiery pain tore through her. The cleaning medicines always seared like fire. Nausea rose and her vision blurred as she fought to keep her eyes open.

Ripping a longer strip of cloth from one of the clean rages she began the painful process of tying the bandage into place. As she finished, she slumped to the ground, sweat dripping from her, fighting to stay alert despite the smouldering in her side.

I have to get up, she focused on that thought. *Get moving. Stay alive.*

Struggling to her feet, she staggered further into the old caves, following the small finger of fresh air that eddied by her in the dark, until she found the entrance.

Only the dark skies of a predawn met her as she climbed out of the cave onto the rugged hillside. Quickly turning, she looked back toward the village. There were only a few flames left dancing in the darkened streets. She found she had no strength left and fell to the rock ledge of the cave. There she watched her world burn away. Darkness claimed here and she did not move until the last few sparks spitting had changed to fingers of curling smoke rising up into the sky.

Morning, or almost, from the stars. How long had she been unconscious? It seemed she had taken much longer than she had anticipated. Even with the healing salves, the wounds still stung, but she had to ignore them.

From this perch, in the early morning light, she could see a faint trail through the grasslands to the south. Her heart swelled with hope as she realized that meant some of the town might have escaped. The trail pointed toward the canyons a half day's journey away. They had hidden food and weapons there and if any reached it there was hope. Some would live. Some had to live!

She turned to the east and saw another track heading away across the half desert toward the dark sea. It was a bold slash of a trail that made no attempt to hide itself telling her who had gone that direction.

So, she thought scanning the landscape, *Mot headed back to his mountain home and he has prisoners.*

He was herding townspeople like cattle to the slaughter. She turned back to the remains of the settlement as a sour morning light illuminated the scene. A weight, heavy as a mountain, settled in the pit of her soul.

Turning toward the east she scrambled down the rock-strewn hillside. The ache in her side a prod as she trudged across the grazing lands. She had to find them. It was not hard to follow the trail of Mot, the beast, and his captured villagers. Their boldness made her anger burn bright and so she followed. Toward the haunting purple hills spread across the distant horizon.

"If you seek out your enemy, your enemy will find you." The voice of Turga repeated in her ears hours later as she was herded forward by some of Mot's men.

She had tracked the group when the marauders caught her. She thought she was keeping low and out of sight but they must have circled around and then caught her between the army ahead and the warriors behind. Cursing herself for a fool she realized her exhaustion and her anger had made her careless.

Now, she too was being herded along. Companion to some of the villagers she had hoped to rescue. Some people recognized her and called out for help as if they could not see she was bound as well.

"We are all prisoners!" she replied lifting her own bound hands.

"What can we do then? There is no hope and we will all surely die!"

"What can we do?" She glared at the people around here. "Live! Do not be a fool. Just live as long as you can! We are not goats to be slaughtered! "

The trek to the dark mountains was endless and they stumbled behind the soldiers of Mot. Sun baked faces stared hopeless as they shuffled trying to keep up with the party.

She knew they did not have much hope. She did not know how many of the others had heard the rumors she had about what the man did with his captives. Mot did not take prisoners to work any fields or tend any herds. There were few slaves living out long lives in his forces. They had been taken from their village for one purpose only. They would feed the fires of sacrifice to Mot's deity of death.

Live! She told herself what she had told so many others. *Just live as long as you can.*

After days of trudging through the heat and trying to sleep in the chill of the night, they reached the shadow draped slopes of Mot's home on Mount Cassius.

Anath had never smelled such a stench in all of her life. The rank odor of death permeated the camp. She had noted the unwashed smell of the raiders but in the open desert the wind had carried most of the scent away. Here the smell hung in the air and she gagged on the stink.

It was impossible to say where the smells came from. There were rotting corpses hung speared on tall wooden stakes. Animal hides lay rotting on the ground covered in maggots. Moist bones piled in tumbled heaps still covered with putrefying meat. Refuse heaps teeming with flies so that the filth seemed to boil and eddy in waves.

Stacks of stones littered the area and she could see an edifice rising at the far end of the camp. Stacks of wood and the black stain of smoke gave her pause. What obscene rites did Mot follow in his bloody religion?

Stepping to avoid dung it was clear that here man and animals relieved themselves when and where they liked. The stench was almost more than she could bear. The cookpots, far too close to the stinking trenches, bubbled with coarse odors that made Anath hope they planned to starve them to death.

As horrible as the camp was above ground, she shivered as they stopped beside a deep hole dug into the ground. A wooden ladder led down into the dark and reeking pit.

Glaring at the shadowy depths she took a deep breath and descended into what she knew must be hell itself.

Asherah watched as the last of the bodies blazed like torches. Around her the sing-song chant of mourning rose and fell. She could feel nothing. Her father and stepmother dead. So many friends horribly butchered or burned as buildings fell. There were so few of them left. So few.

She refused to believe that Anath was dead. The others did not believe she lived but they could not feel her inside the way Asherah did.

There was much work to be done. She was torn between a desire to stay and the need to protect the people who remained. "Come Melqart, we must gather those who can still fight."

"What is the use?" He spoke listlessly as he hobbled on his one good leg. His wives and children had been taken and his spirit was gone. "We can never match them in number or skills. In the mountains they have all the advantage."

"They could not have traveled fast with that group of prisoners. They have no doubt just reached the mountain trails."

"It has been too many days Asherah. While we struggled to find one another and to recover they reached the mountains. You know the stories of what they do; I cannot ride with this leg and I cannot walk! They will be dead long before I could ever reach them or any here." He flashed a look at her filled with pain. "They may be dead already."

"Until I see the body of Anath, I will believe there is hope. I urge you to do the same for your wife and children. There is still hope that we can have our revenge on Mot. "

"Then you are a fool or a mad woman."

"That may be true. Either way, I will not sit here and be food for the ravens." She turned away and knew that she feared that his words were all too true. "Anath! We need you. I need you!"

From the way her head pounded the next morning, Anath suspected they had been drugged. At least, she felt more rested, whatever the cause of the sleep. Every day was the same as they waited. She overheard the guards talking of some special feast day that approached. Newcomers seemed to arrive each day and she suspected the prisoners were going to be the main entertainment when the great day finally arrived.

Every few hours their captors forced them to drink more of a bitter juice and she knew they were giving them something to make them sleep. She tried to spit it out and was hit in the side with a staff. If someone did not drink their fill, a boot held them on the ground and the foul stuff was forced down their throat.

In one of the brief moments of awareness between dosing's, she realized that she had not had any dreams. That meant no contact with her sister and no rescue. Feeling alone she grasped the desperation that had driven some of the people had taken their own lives.

One night, a great cheer arose in the camp, and through the haze of sleep she realized the rest of the raiders had finally arrived. New prisoners were added but they were merely vague shapes moving in the darkness. She could hear nothing and she could barely move. All she wanted to do at that moment was die herself.

The next day, as drums pounded a dreadful rhythm that made her head ache, they were brought out of the stinking pits. Squinting in the sudden harsh light she made out little of the surroundings at first. An acrid aroma hung over the camp and in the distance a hazy smoky fire reached in the sky. Guards grated harsh orders and herded them toward where a noisy throng gathered at the heart of the camp. There, whirling around the mound's center, where the fires scorched, Mot's people swayed to the awful beat of those drums.

Pressed forward, she nearly stumbled, and as she righted herself she was close enough to see the drums clearly. Turning away she realized sickly they were covered in human skin.

Anath coughed in the harsh smoke hanging heavily in the air and realized it was not natural. That dense swirling fog was untouched by the winds. Despite the intense heat caused by the grasping flames she shivered but was forced ahead. Struggling with the leather strips around her wrists, Anath, tried to free herself but was booted by one of the guards.

The center of the encampment had been transformed by raised platforms and the space filled with a rowdy mass of people. A bellows fanned the fires near something that looked like a huge altar. The growl of the flames from its pit was like roaring animal with the steady drum beat its thundering heart. The air was filled with heat and the aroma of death. The hazy unnatural smoke making it hard to see details. As the miasma moved, and she could see more clearly, what she saw froze her heart.

The fixed drum beat changed then, indicating something was about to happen and all eyes shifted to focus on the raised platform. On the top of the long structure three figures appeared between guards. She recognized them.

"God, no!" Anath cried and lunged forward only to be prodded with a club to the ground.

Anath watched in horror as Melqart's wife and daughters were dragged up the sides of the makeshift temple. The flames from the offering pit were like scarlet tipped hands pawing, probing, and eager to gobble up the innocents.

"No!" Anath struggled again but the guards held her down. "No!"

Kama, her eyes wild with terror, hung back struggling valiantly screaming for her babies to run. That was impossible because the arms of the men who followed were locked around their tiny bodies.

Ina, the older at six, was silent as if aware of her fate. Little Thatha was upset at her Mother's cries, and the strange place, and flailed her arms and legs

Anath gasped and could not scream so deep was her pain. Tears spilled onto her cheeks as she watched Melqart's young bride pushed forward. She jerked fiercely at the bounds and struggling to escape the clutch of Mot's men.

Kama was yanked toward a platform as two priests came forward. They wore the horrible masks made to look like faces distorted in pain and twisted into forms like monsters.

Chest heaving another man stepped forward and tore his mask off to a loud cheer. Mot's face. Arms raised in a victorious salute he strode around the dais accepting the acclaim of the crowd. Swords, pounding against shields, took up the pounding rhythm of the drums. As the man finished his arrogant spectacle, the priests finally dragged the woman toward the gaping maw, where hungry flames stretched out eagerly probing.

"No!" Anath watched in horror as they threw Kama into the pit. At her harsh screams, the crowd seemed to grow even wilder surging against the steps. They tore at their clothes and sliced into their flesh so it ran crimson with their blood. All around there was a frenzy of depravity as men and women began to move in openly all around her. They tore at their clothes and stretched out bony gasping hands as if to tear her apart.

Like wild beasts they turned on one another with raw screams and the sounds of death. She shut her eyes tight to block out the horrific sights.

Above the clamouring noise of the crowd, she heard a laugh she knew from children and the sound chilled her to the bone. The throaty laugh of Hadad. She had heard news he called himself Bel and she had refused to believe he would go so low as to join with these people.

Snapping her head around she searched across the crowd and finally found him. Standing by the platform, dressed much as Mot and the priests, he laughed at the spectacle. *Laughed!*

"Hadad! Listen, Hadad!" Her cries were lost in the roar of the crowd around her. She yanked on the restraints holding her but the man nearest her cuffed her across the face. Dazed, she licked the blood from her mouth, and sought out her brother once more. She was shoved forward once more; closer to the horrors of the flames.

She did not have time to think any more as she saw the men moving forward toward the fire pit. She had witnessed the revulsion of seeing Kama, sweet gentle girl that she was, tossed to those hungry flames. Anath dreaded as the men herded her nieces forward.

No, she silently prayed feeling her bones turn to water at the horror, *not that too.*

Shocked awareness had carved lines of terror into their tiny faces. They looked like stone as a one of the men ran forward with a cup. After forcing the liquid down them he tossed the cup into the fire to roaring cheers. The small bodies collapsed.

"Thank you," Anath breathed, praying theirs was a painless poison. "Thank you for that small mercy."

Then she saw Hadad watching from the side, beaming and shouting with the others, and she struggled to her feet. One of the guards yanked on her chains then and she turned on him. He retreated instinctively faced with such snarling ferocity as she saw on her face.

"No!" Her voice screamed across the square. "Hadad! Stop this!"

The roar of the people drowned out her sudden cries. When the two men reached out and raised the bodies of her nieces high above their heads to show the crowd, she strained at the straps holding until blood seeped down her wrists.

She shrieked, as they were tossed into the fiery maw like tiny broken branches, and it was such a long raw cry that she felt her throat rip and bleed.

Swaying in the sudden loss, her pain was worse than any beating, and it sprang from some bloodied and awful place deep within her soul. She sagged, and nearly fell, as she trudged forward.

The crowd with its incessant cries, the monstrous beating heart of the drums, and the hellish heat of the fire, and bloody hunger worse than any wild beast. Her own fate faded into the background as a thousand scenes swirled through her head: Kama laughing, her brother lifting Thatha high to twirl her around with a laugh, and shy little Ina hiding from strangers. All of these merged with what she had just seen. Falling heavily to her knees then she was overcome at last. The light from the pit drew her gaze but she did not really see the pit. Tall crimson flames licked hungrily into the sky, stretching with a gruesome covetousness, and she felt the ashes of the life, sloughed away in a dreadful furnace.

She drew herself up to her feet then to face her fate as a warrior. Deep inside of her something died and she felt something else, some terrible purpose, stir to ravenous life.

Her keepers pulled hard on the leather straps and the chains binding her. Surprising she was led, not down toward the fire with the other captives, but away from the main camp area. Moving fast she was half-dragged into shadowed halls carved deep into the rock hillside.

The cool of air of the cave caused her to shiver as she was led further into its shadowed interior. Through holes and fissures in the rocks she had glimpses of darker recesses or sight of the distant desert.

Outside were horrors too awful to contemplate while here was a realm suitable for a prince. Soft curtains on walls rippled in the breeze. Tapestries danced around the entrances in bold splashes of deep red and black. Strange markings painted the rock walls.

Her guards shoved her down into the room and struggled to her feet to turn on glare at them. They ignored her as they stalked off to take positions outside the entrance. Left on her own, hands still bound, she searched for a way to escape but only found the one entrance. Frustrated, she scouted the area for something sharp enough to cut through her bonds or to help her flee. Nothing but heaps of cushions and animal skins. Nothing!

Her eyes were pulled back to the symbols on the walls. They told a tale. *Can they tell me anything that might help me escape or fight these monsters?* Any tool would help...

Scanning the images closer, keeping one eye on the hallway and the guards, some of it began to make some sense. Their stark angles and scenes told stories of death and horror. Nausea rose, and the scenes outside were fresh in her mind, and now seeing how there was such glory in chaos, blood, and death. The people who followed this Mot were not human. They were worse than animals. She knew now they were worse, far worse, than the tales carried to by the rare survivors.

"If they worship death," she whispered, "they are fouler than even the worst nightmares." *I should have listened when the warriors, Augum and Hayak especially, tried to warn me.*

A sound spun her around. Two women, squat round women of some years, entered from the within the caverns. Gesturing, hands pointing into the interior, they indicated she should come with them.

Pulling back the coverings along one wall they revealed an opening and led her further into the dark caves. In an inner nook, several woman poured jars of water into a basin cut into the floor. Others hurried over to her chattering away in different tongues; all Mot's followers appeared to be from a variety of foreign peoples.

One the women turned towards her roughly ripping away her clothes. She struggled and hit out at the women. Then she realized they meant her to bathe. Clothes were laid out nearby. She had seen the type of women who wore that thin tunic and those ornaments.

"No! Get away from me!" Had Mot traded her away as some brothel whore! Was this some obscene sacred rite before she too met the flames or some worse death?

She began to struggle anew, and one of the women whistled and suddenly the women surrounded her, pushing her into the water. Hands harshly washed away the filth and grime of the days in that stinking pit.

Sputtering and glaring she was able to stand as they stepped back. She tugged the clothes out of their hands and turned her back to begin dressing. Under no circumstances would she be dressed like an infant too weak to fend for herself. Not in the camp of her enemies. It was bad enough that they had bathed her, oiled her, and scented her like a field of flowers.

The women took her back to the other room where she had been left. A sudden girlish giggling had her turning around. Her brother strode in and the women continued to ogle and giggle as they hurried out.

"I see you have been refreshed." Hadad walked over to a low table and picked up a cup there. The glint of gold and its style revealed its value. He tipped it up and took a long drink from its contents. He held the cup gently as if savoring its feel in his hands. Strange creatures chased each other around the rim, jaws dripping blood. *A beastly creation for a beastly man,* she thought.

"How could you?" She demanded. She resisted the urge to hide behind her hands. She felt naked but in the sheer clothes but she would not be made small by any man.

"The gods demand great sacrifices for great rewards." He sipped more of the wine. "The greater the gift the more honor is won."

"What kind of a *God* demands such a high price? Your own brother's wife and his children, Hadad, how could you!"

"Bel! The name is Bel; do not forget it woman!" His voice rang in the chamber. In a calmer voice he added, "He will have other wives now. If Mot allows him to live. There will be many other children. Only sons; we keep only sons here." He told her. "They will all be fine warriors. From them we will create a nation of mighty heroes!"

He came closer. "I remember when father brought your Mother home. I hated her and I hated him. My Mother had died only the winter before and then *she* came crawling out of the desert. Soon there was a squalling girl child as well and then your sister. Then another wife and meek Malqart!"

"Malqart's mother was kind to you!"

"And that is why he lives to spawn sons. Had he been Dagon, or any of a number of others, I would have killed him without thought."

"Your father loved you very much."

"He abandoned me!" Hadad said with a growl as he tossed away his cup.

"Never! Why, tell me, why do you suddenly hate us all so much?"

"You are weak. Your gods are weak." The voice was Hadad's but it was said in a strange tone. As if he did not speak at all. "They accomplish nothing."

"You were once part of us, Hadad."

"I am Bel now. Hadad is dead. Yes, I was once part of you. Year after I year I watched as we grew soft and meek. We were once as harsh as this land!"

"You were once a kind brother, a loving son, and a true friend. You talk of growing hard by murder. These acts do not make a people strong! The people and the land are weakened by these things."

"Anath you are so wrong. I thought like you once. I was too young to grasp what the gods were telling me even then."

"You lived in harmony and you knew peace."

"The endless and unchanging boredom of peace. How I hated that! I needed the thunder and the wind and the rain that ripped away and made everything new. The storm called to me even then!"

She looked at the man before her and saw a stranger. That man she had known was dead and a demon filled his skin.

"You are mad just like that killer, Mot!"

"There are people in the high mountains and at the other side of the desert who have been there since the time before time. Do you know that?" His eyes looked at something only he could see and his voice was casual as if he were discussing a meal. "They are hard as rock. No weakness is found among them. They live to fight and they find death their wine."

"Please Hadad…Bel…let me go!" She appealed to him. Was there some tiny part of the man she knew hidden in there still? He turned away and she saw the incisions in his flesh. The marks of Mot were already on him. "You can end all this! Let me go!"

"Those people remember well the gardens that once flourished in this desert. They can recount the tales of how new gods robbed them of the rivers." He looked beyond her, his eyes focused on some other place she could not see. "Gods who were soft, planting fields and watching herds, instead of taking what they needed. That life ended. I have heard their songs of when the water was not so far away. Such haunting melodies…"

"Hadad, Bel, listen to me. Don't you remember how we were once family?" she asked. Perhaps, if he could remember, and with that memory he might regain his sanity. "We played in the hillsides. You can't have forgotten all of that!"

"That is just what I am saying now, sister. You are not listening! They were prophecies of our future those stories, not poems about our past!"

Hadad really is gone, she thought as she followed him with her eyes, *leaving only this creature.* She hoped, perhaps too much, that he could be reached and the brother she had known would re-emerge.

"We are those new gods and we will push you and your old, weak gods into the furnace." He pulled her closer and the way he looked at her made her squirm anew. She struggled but his hold was so strong. "Death will win as it must always win. We ride to drive you all into the heart of the desert and into the furnace of disorder."

He dipped his head then, breathing deeply of the oils they had poured over her body, and his grip changed. His voice changed as he whispered into her hair: "Those stories also told of a god who married his sister."

"You are mad! Mot has turned your mind with his blood thirst." This was not the brother who taught her to ride or the brother who helped her in so many ways.

"Isn't it? I was riding one day as a thunderstorm roared about me. I was reckless and searching for answers. If I died, well, that would also be my answer. There was nothing. No fingers of light speared me as I rode. In fact, the storm seemed to answer my call. I knew then. I was special. I had a destiny!"

"It would have been better if you had died than. Better than hearing you talk as you are now. This is madness."

"No, I am in my right mind and for the first time in my life!"

"You talk of murder as if asking for a grape or piece of bread. That is madness." Anath gritted her teeth, glaring up at Hadad. "What is the use? Just stop talking and kill me! Kill me now!"

"I do not want to kill you, little sister. You do not understand what the gods revealed to me, but you will. You must. Mot showed me this and it made so much sense. You must live here and you must become my wife. You see, there is no one else, in the whole world, worthy to bear my child."

"No. That is impossible!" Anath cried out. "We are brother and sister."

"No. We are not that. We merely shared a home for a while as close kin. My father was not yours and your mother was not mine. There is no taboo, Anath."

He pulled her close again and she backed away, blindly seeking escape, and into something solid and unmoving.

Two hands grasped her shoulders halting her retreat. She saw Hadad pull to a stop with a dark scowl, fists opening and closing at his sides, and a muscle rippling in his neck.

Twisting around slightly, she looked into the eyes of Mot, and froze like a spider staring at a scorpion. His eyes were odd; dark pools with strange shots of white like lightening. As she watched, there was a bizarre spiralling movement in their depths and a chill ran over her body. The room seemed darker as if filled with a silken fog, dark as night, and then she noticed the fog was hugging his form. A rippling shadow of hazy fog that caused her to push away from his grasp. His lip curled in a small movement as if her reactions amused him. Mot moved so suddenly she was shoved forward, stumbling. She spun around, warily, keeping them both in view.

Releasing her, he went to the table and poured out some wine. Dark and ruby toned as blood, it smelled of spices and honey, and he drank deeply. Lowering the cup, he examined the younger man. "My dear friend do you seek to enjoy the richest treasure all alone?" Mot's voice was low and rough. It had a strange enthralling quality to it, though, that pulled at the mind. She shook her head to ward off the sensation. "Or, perhaps you bring me a gift?"

That was when she saw Hadad sway slightly. He turned to the source of the voice but his eyes did not appear to focus. Anath caught her breath as an odd nimbus of the smoky fog seemed to wrap feathery fingers around Hadad. There was a flutter of wings, a gust of air rush past and she was sure she saw a dark bird meld into the shadows. Then one thin twisting finger of the fog speared into his skull. An odd glazed look slide down over his face and his features went slack.

What evil was this? Her sister had warned that Mot used some obscure magic. This was unlike anything she had ever seen. A chill rippled over her skin as the room filled with the strange hazy fog. The seemed alive. They broke into pieces spilling all across the room. They darted and flew past.

Mot's eyes caught her glance, she could not move, and as she watched his eyes blazed like bright embers. Unable to move she realized there was dangerous terrain all around She had to be cautious until she had puzzled it out.

Then it was all gone. The air was clear and everything was free of any taint or lingering sense of an evil presence. As if he were a toy flung aside by a thoughtless child, Hadad lost his balance and caught himself against the wall. Mumbling, or merely cursing under his breath, her brother turned away stumbling awkwardly to a cushion. He seemed to diminish as he collapsed, losing all interest in all of his surroundings. His eyes unfocused and his skin ashen as if he had died long days before.

Mot poured another cup of wine as if no one else was in the room.

"What have you done to him?"

"He is merely tired after all the excitement of the day."

"There is a spell, some conjuring, of yours at work here!"

"Spells are for old women and small children." He grabbed her. A groan escaped at the malicious bite of his hard, cold hands. There was an animal like musk that filled her senses and she pushed against him. His fingers cut into her flesh. "It is the magic, the deep and powerful magic, of the oldest gods!"

"I know all I need to know about your God! Your god is cruel! A vicious monster and not a god!" She spat out, thinking of her poor nieces. He pulled her to him and felt his fingers dig deeper into her flesh. "That is not magic but madness."

"You and your kind are all weak. Mine is the magic of the great and wonderful gods of blood and death! Only in them is there any truth or meaning to life. Death is the welcome release from this life!" Lifting the medallion from her neck he examined it. "There is so much you do not know. This around your neck hints at how much you are like me. My Gods. You are closer to us than you think, warrior."

"Never! Your way is only death and destruction. You are animals parading as men!"

He raised his knife and slit the leather cord and yanked the medallion from her throat and held it high in one muscled hand. The other hand kept a hard grip on her arm.

"These are the real Gods, woman! Not your puny spirits of amity and love. Here, among my people, there are real gods who walk in the shadows and who have always walked there. They speak through the rotting bones of their enemies. Do you feel their power drawing you? Listen now. Hear the wind, and whispering sounds from the darkness. They are calling to you to be one with them!"

Anath tried to jerk away from him but he held her too firmly. She cast a desperate glance to where Hadad still sat. He was still in a trance. There was nothing left there she could reach and no help. Mot's grip twisted, his sharp fingernails digging fiercely into her flesh, bringing more blood. "You are a demon who feeds on gore! Let me go!"

She hated feeling so powerless!

"I am no demon. I am a man, still. Perhaps one day...." Suddenly the black haze was sinuously winding around them, around Mot. He marched her across the room. She darted another despairing look toward where Hadad still sat staring like a statue.

"You will find no help there! Your brother is my faithful attendant. He sees to my needs in so many important ways." Suddenly he was so close that she felt it difficult to breath. It was as if a monstrous beast had risen from the shadows. The fog and the wrapped massive bonds of muscle and flesh enveloped her. The spiced oils of his skin mingled so she felt her head begin to spin and it was hard to stand. "Some needs, however, are beyond the ability of even the most faithful hound."

More revolting enchantments from a creature who passed himself off as a man. She looked around for escape but the air was filled with the overwhelming stench of burning spices that made her weak.

"Let me go! No!" She struggled but seemed to be unable to fight off the effects of whatever magic was being used. "Get away from me!"

"Come," he said half pushing and half dragging her across the room. Past the staring form of her brother he dragged her and shoved her through the pale hangings into darkness. Behind them the draperies fluttered like the eager wings of carrion surrounding the remains of her hope.

"Let me introduce you to his priest...."

Chapter 18

The screams were a shrill cry of pain and torment that echoed through rock cold corridors. The sound so sharp she sat up from sleep and then clutched her head as the sound faded. With its passing a throbbing began. Holding her aching head she realized the dream cries that had awakened her had been had been her own.

Her eyes barely responded despite her desire to open them. What she saw was blurred and hesitantly her fingers explored the tender skin around the eyes. They were nearly swollen shut and a thick crust of blood around the one sealed it tightly closed. Her memories of the night before were a hazy blur. One pain following closely after another.

That hideous thick smoke filled and the odor of those bizarre spices had quickly made her dizzy. The aroma had made her feel weak and the scenes around her became disjointed. *"Let me introduce you to his priest...."*

After that, her memory was full of holes. She had no idea how long she had been in this new pit. No way of knowing anything except it had the same stink of rotting filth and her body ached with pain. Below it all was something even worse, an oily film of evil that soured the very air with its presence.

It reminded her what she had encountered once deep in a cavern where an old bear had lived and died. It was a fetid odor of wild beasts, dank pelt, and other tainted unseen things. Whatever it was, it mirrored all of the awful horrors she had experienced as prisoner.

Sitting in the dark, the smell of the earth all around her, and the smoke of the death fires still hanging in the air, she felt as if she was already dead and in her tomb.

Small bits of memory rose like filth on water to taunt her with what she had done and what they had done to her. *"A warrior captured takes all, lives through all, and fights another day."* The words of Turga floated to the surface of her mind. It was a beacon to give her direction. She clutched at it in the darkness and prayed to survive to have her vengeance.

Strangely, she had expected they would have would have soon finished with her and herded her down to the fire pit for sacrifice. Instead of that furnace ditch, they dragged her to this rough dark prison pit they had carved down into the side of a hill. What did they hope to gain? As the door closed behind her each time, locking her inside the dark rock womb, she wondered when her death would happen.

She focused on her training and rehearsed in her mind the lessons she had learned. She rehearsed plans and discarded them as useless for long hours. Her chances were all slim and depended as much on luck and daring as skill.

Now, as a sickly dawn light trickled into the hall, she heard someone coming. She sat up and flexed her sore muscles.

"Here is food." The door creaked open and one of the men, one she had not seen before, swatted down to slid in a wooden tray. She barely glanced at the dry bread and even drier looking goat's cheese.

He looked young. Inexperienced.

"Please," she croaked. "Help me please! I am so thirsty." Silently, she went closer to the door. Her raspy voice was not artifice but she tried to make it sound weaker. Pleading as well. "Please, please, just a little water…"

Hesitating, the youth turned back to the hall leaving the door ajar. As he did so, she sprang up. Forcing her body to respond to her commands she gripped his throat with her arm and closed it like a vise around his neck.

Squeezing tightly she pressed him forward. *Visions of Kama laughing and then screaming as she fell into the flames filled her head.* He kicked and tried to move her arm at his throat. He swung fits at her and grunting she endured when they connected. *Little Ina chasing a butterfly in the garden.* She pushed and pulled with all of her strength until his body was down. Until she was on her knees and he was struggling, desperately, to get up. *The children high atop that altar as the flames licked upwards towards them.* She squeezed until she felt her own bones would break and then tightened her arm even more.

He sagged suddenly and slumped lifelessly to the floor. She kept her grip on his neck. She had to be sure he would not raise an alarm. Finally releasing him, she shoved the weight away from her. She drank in deep gulps of air. Flexing aching muscles in her hands she straightened and listened.

Moving as quickly as she could, with every movement causing her muscles to scream, she removed his thick cotton shift and shrugged it over her head. Quickly, she strapped on the leather boots and laced them as tight as she could.

He carried no weapons but he did have a wide thick belt. It went around her waist several times but it would serve to protect her. She stuffed the dry bread and cheese into a pouch hanging on a wall.

Tugging off his leather helmet she pulled if down over her own head. With her fingers, she hid her longer hair. She would pass if someone did not came too close. From a distance, in his tunic and his helmet, the others might think she was one of them.

Dragging his lifeless body deeper into the shadows of her own cell, she propped him up, and set the food tray by the door. With luck, this might work. Stepping as lightly as she could, she crept into the hall, down the passage, and paused at the entrance before she finally dashed out. Once free of the area she turned sharply to hide as she moved through the early dawn shadows.

In moments, she was far away from the prison, moving out of the camp. As the dawn turned to mid-day, she was miles from the site, following animal trails to keep out of view.

Finally, though, as the day began to soften into night, she slept. She had lived through the last days and, although she did not know what the next might bring, she knew one thing with certainty.

"You made a mistake not to kill me." She spoke into the fading darkness seeing two faces. For justice for those killed, she was now duty bound to seek revenge. She pushed down the memories of Hadad as a distant but tolerant older brother. The images of Kama and her children she locked away into a distant corner of her mind.

Instead, she fixed the face Hadad, now Bel and of his demon mentor, Mot. Those she would not forget.

She flexed muscles and grimaced as the pains shot through her body. She touched her neck where Mot had torn her Mother's medallion from her.

"Yes, you made a very grave mistake."

Chapter 19

As Anath walked across the bare sands, time lost meaning, and the days merged into one long journey of heat and light. Reaching the horizon, where the dry river channel would lead her back to her home, she paused and turned. A small column of white dust rose into the morning air.

She had known they would follow. In her heart, she knew it would be Hadad. He had too much to lose with his new demigod, Mot. When she rested at night, she did not sleep long, because she sensed the men followed.

The brother she had known was dead. Hadad was now *Bel,* he worshipped the chaos and the death Mot achieved with each breath he took. She had heard stories of ancient battles and mighty deeds. Always the themes of justice, revenge, and honor drove those heroes to victory. She had no illusions of riches and honor to prod her. There were only images seared into her memory of innocence sacrificed into greedy savage flames.

She wept as memories surfaced of a time of sweetness long past and the loss cut into her with the sharpness of a blade. No one would ever hear those gentle voices. No one would know what gifts those babes would have given to the people.

Sparks, red and gold, shot high into the dark sky dancing on eddies and swaying to a silent piper. Covered in gory ashes, Mot stood naked before the blazing fire, and felt the sweat running down his lean body. In the darkness hugging close, there was a swirling cloud of living shadows, and he could feel their hot breath caressing his body. They were dancing and curving around his frame and as each smoky tendril brushed against his skin, he gasped.

It was working! He was one with the beast! He shuddered as the beast loped up the hillside; he was one with it and seeing all it saw.

The connection was stronger this time. The creature not only took him into his mind but they shared a bond to destroy. Since he had attacked the first town, in response to Mot's bidding, the link between them had become more powerful.

He licked his lips at the sudden tastes filling his being. The tang of warm blood spurting into his mouth and the teeth tearing into hunks of raw flesh; they were *his* teeth biting into that meat! It was *his* mouth tasting the blood! His body shuddered in the mounting surge of sensation flowing over and through his being. It was all his now…his to control and command.

All because of the medallion worn by that whore Anath. It had been by accident that he had learned of its tremendous power. An image of Anath flashed through his mind. She had glared at him when he had taken the medallion. Had she had the power that day her eyes alone could have killed him. The stories of her Mother, and her strangeness, had traveled as far as the deep canyons where his people had lived. As soon as he had seen the carvings etched into it he had known it was destined to be his.

His thumb traced the strange carvings once more. He traced the sinuous lines with one finger and marveled what other powers were locked within. She had escaped before he had wrested everything she knew about the object. Their secrets would be his soon enough anyway.

The beast touched his mind then he threw back his head as hot power flowed through him like wild tongues of fire burning and melting his very bones. His entire body shuddered with the feeling of the connection to the creature.

The old one in the mountains had cautioned him that the creature might become too strong to handle. He had gibbered on and on about tales of men who had sought to rein in chaos but instead embraced death sooner than they had imagined. Bah! Old fools afraid of their own shadows!

Mot *knew* he was different.

"I am a child of death, born of a dead woman, and set apart for some great task!" His voice stirred the dancing sparks. He had already proven he was not feeble like others around him. He had the will to act as needed. When still just a child he had slain his own father to insure the prosperity of his people. They would still be there, huddled in dank valley caves, except for him. His was a destiny of greatness.

Sudden exhaustion, however, caused him to sink to the ground. There was a price to be paid for such overwhelming power. The unrelenting waves of awareness were strenuous.

Even as he sank into the sands he wanted more and he craved it like a warm heady wine. He ached for that link and the power he felt through the monster. Closing his eyes he saw again the flashes of forest through the eyes of the creature. He felt the sharp rocks cutting into bare feet and harsh panting breath drummed in his ears.

He leaped up suddenly and nervously paced the darkness. He was filled with a desperate hunger for hot blood spouting from torn flesh. His hand raised, fingers curled like claws, as he watched they seemed to change in the dying firelight. Flesh shifted to new forms, fingers elongated, and twisted in unnatural shapes with talon like nails.

A humming began somewhere around him, like a swarm of flies, growing louder and louder. The sound seemed inside his head. The hum was now a roar. The pain!

"No! I am in control!" He screamed into the darkness. "I am in control!"

Jerking off the medallion, he flung it to the ground, and his hands returned to their familiar shape. The link had already begun to diminish. He looked at the medallion and then picked it up to hold it in his hand. He would need to keep it off until he grew stronger. He had to learn more of how its magic worked and how to insure his mastery of the beast. The beast was still there in his head though…more distant as it prowled the dark hillsides …but still there.

"I am in control! I am in control!" Why did he sound like a frightened child? He was Mot! Still, he knelt back into the sand and pulled the medallion closer to him. With this, he had control of the beast. He would just need the secret of its control. Once he had control of the beast he would master the world. Master the world and then destroy it.

He was coming. She saw the lone horseman riding hard. Though miles separated them she knew who it was. She turned aside, marked the position of the sun, and then waited for him. "I will speak for them and my words will be sharp and strong…"

They would fight and he would die. She had sworn that to the memory of those he had killed and those he allowed to die.

The unrelenting heat beat on her and she remembered as a child watching a sword made. She saw the hot metal removed from the fires and the hammer beating against it forming it and making it strong. The steam as the metal was thrust into the water to strengthen it for use.

As the days dragged on, and she pushed herself, she had realized this was her furnace. The girl Anath had died long ago, far away in those pits, in the dark nights of pain. The hammer blows had been fierce and merciless but she was taking new form. Not merely a warrior but as a weapon in every fiber of her being.

In the full light, as he neared, she could plainly his sinewy muscles worked as he spurred the horse toward her. They were like hard ropes of leather.

What did he see, she wondered briefly? Did she have that same lean, hungry look of an animal? She hoped he could foretell his death when he looked at her waiting for him.

He rode at her hard on the back of Cloudrider. He leaped off the horses with a snarl. He knocked her down but she slipped away. Jumping to her feet, gripping the short sword she had taken from the young guard, she lashed out at him.

Hadad, or now Bel, was an animal. Frothing and bellowing like a sick bull he slashed wildly at her. Blindly he jabbed at her with his sword.

She easily evaded his anger driven moves. Hadad had never devoted time to practice and often slept during lessons. Discipline had never been a strength with her brother. It was always easier to run off with his friends than spend time practicing on the training grounds. He cried out as her blade sliced into his arm.

She doubted the man he had become had changed in these last years. Mot's world seemed to be one of destruction, gratification and desire. None of those were forces that sharpened a knife to do its work. In Mot's world, the tools would be left to rust in the rains. She had seen their camps. They did no work; they destroyed, robbed and then discarded with equal ease. She jabbed and he jerked as the blade slide along his side and crimson blood curtained down his flank.

She allowed him to swing at her again, wearing him out, as she easily dodged his thrusts. Calling out, she taunted him so his anger continued to climb like a stoked fire.

His way with the sword was crude. Her guess had been right. His temperament had been one of play, quick anger, and mostly hurt feelings. Now he slashed, jabbed, and stabbed but without thought and without plan. He had no balance and her quick moves often left him confused. It was time to end it now.

Stepping aside as he swatted at her with his blade, she twisted around, and drove her sword into his stomach.

"For Kama!"

She withdrew it as he grunted and slashed into his side, "For Ina!"

He fell to his knees gripping his gut.

A final slash across his throat and he slumped over into the sand. "For little Thatha!"

She stooped over his body and yanked the medallion from around his neck. It was the one stolen from her by Mot. She wiped the blood on his skirt before she straightened.

"This is mine," she whispered as she slipped it over her neck and turned away. She slid her sword back into its holder and scanned the area. The other riders had stayed at a distance but now they raced away. No doubt carrying the news of her victory to Mot. Cloudrider had bounded away as the confrontation had started. Riding held no interest for Anath. She turned her face toward the sun and began to walk.

She had no home.

Her family was dead.

She walked: her compass was grief, her map her sorrow, and nowhere her destination.

The sun was an angry one-eyed god burning the land like the fire consumed the sacrifices. The huge mound holding the blackened fire pit and the crude temple had risen on the plains over many seasons with laborers stolen from nearly every land around them.

Mot marveled, as he always did, at the speed with which chaos was consuming the land. It had been only months since Anath had escaped and Hadad had been killed by his loving sister. Those had been minor delays in the larger plan.

How long, he wondered, had the great god of destruction planned and plotted as he waited for a prophet? Mot lifted his head to the skies feeling the scalding wind rake his face. As the dark god waited for Mot – his prophet- Mot had waited for the dark god to ratify his role.

His raids over these years had not been just for a few pretty trinkets. He had sought out people with skills needed to create what he envisioned. He had plundered to find the supplies and ingredients needed for his mission as emissary of the dark god.

Deep in the dank belly of the mound, he came to the chamber he had made for the beast. He motioned away the guards and they scurried away like timid rats. Even as merciless as his men could be, the beast sent them running. Chained and caged it still radiated death. There in that rank darkness it waited, slumbering almost, until he called it forth.

Holding the torch in one hand, he ran his hand over the sacred symbols of spirals and waves incised into the walls. Powerful marks, they were older than the stars or the dirt under his feet. Their secrets had been lost to most of the world but not to Mot.

He remembered when he had first seen them. He remembered when he first learned of them from the strange old man lost in the dry river canyon. The man's screams echoed through the empty gorge but he finally gave up all he knew about the symbols carved on his body.

Mot had never heard of such powers outside of the tales around a campfire. Such power could be his for the taking. Tracing the shapes on the old man's body with the tip of his knife he sliced off the flesh for tanning. He would need a record of their forms if he were to use their power. As he thought of their meaning, he turned away ignoring the dying screams of the man.

For days, he had kept the old man alive wresting from him every drop of knowledge. The man had died but Mot had a taste for the secrets he had been given. He ignored the man's ranting of a land destroyed by such worship. What master wants to share his skills? The shamans and holy ones always claimed some great disaster should they share the secrets. Few, however, could withstand the sharp end of a blade as it peeled them like a piece of fruit.

The encounter had been pivotal for him. He had been a youth when he found that man and first prayed to his god of chaos.

That dark being had answered him!

He had been so shocked when he first heard the swelling hum, like bees released from a hive swirling around him and filling him. There had been pain; such sweet pain that racked him and destroyed him but when he rose he was no longer just Mot.

He rose from that place of death resurrected into one chosen. He had lifted arms high and shouted at being greatly honored by the immense god. He could hardly stand as the air before him ripped and such dark fingers of mist and fog poured out to wrap themselves around him.

His quest to find the knowledge of the beast and make it his own was his only focus. The medallion Hadad had taken was a minor loss; he had copied all it symbols and would soon learn all of its secrets.

He had summoned the creature and hunted through it until the ground was dark with blood. Now, at his command, it waited in this dark place to do his bidding.

He walked closer to the opening and his steps were silent on the dirt floor. There were no doors for no gate could hold this beast. He was chained to the stone wall and held in place by blood incantations and the raw power of chaos. He remained as Mot commanded.

It had been a struggle at first, the beast wanted to be in control, but Mot had sought out way to control the monster. There could only be one master and Mot knew that it must be him.

As he watch, the beast's shaggy head sagged and its breath came in grunting gusts that echoed loudly in the chamber. The stench was strong and brought to mind fields of slaughter and old blood.

A humming began somewhere around him, like a swarm of flies, growing louder and louder. The sound seemed inside his head. The hum was now a roar.

He glanced sharply at the beast and it was staring at him, his jaws open, black saliva dripping from them in thick glistening ropes. A long black tongue slide across his lips and he showed his teeth, bits of rotting flesh hanging there. He looked at Mot with such intensity that Mot stepped back.

"Bow your head to me!" Mot screamed at him. "Bow it or I will wear your hide for a vest!"

Instead of meekly lowering that massive head, he twitched his shoulders, and began a slow shuffle toward where Mot stood.

"Back beast! The god of chaos commands!"

Still it came steadily forward. Eyes glowed red in the darkness.

The hum was back as well, growing and pressing against his head like a vise. Mot backed away feeling the nausea rise in him.

Something he could not see, but as sharp as an auger, bored into his head. The pain was almost more than he could withstand. Massive paws, tipped with those long claws, reached out to him. They pawed and clutched at the air with a deadly force and need.

Up from the festering ground rose a fetid stench filled fog. The mist swirled between the beast and Mot. It formed a wall like barrier and the beast fell back with an angry grunt and a bellow like roar.

"Why do you desert me - ?" Mot mumbled as the pain in his head intensified. "I serve only you…only you."

The fog remained low hugging the ground, dark and foul, but in the background, the humming went on. It tunneled into his head and seemed to gnaw at his bones. The agony was more than he could endure. There was a sound of cloth ripping or flesh tearing that filled the chamber.

The agony was a fire rippling through his bones. Each breathe was a tortured struggle. Suddenly, he began to laugh and could not stop. His cackle was like thunder to his ears and sounded like the chortle of a mad man.

Mot backed his bleeding body up until he felt the rough rock of the passageway. The pressure lessoned as he turned and ran trying to escape yet having a mad desire to run back and offer himself to that monster. "The beast is not mine," he panted as he sped drunkenly down the dark passageway, he realized his god had tricked him. "The beast was never been mine to command."

He was not the chosen one of the god despite his planning. *That* creature was the hand of the god of death. *It* was the true weapon of chaos.

"I have been tricked!" He felt the laughter spill over once more. As he rushed out into the open air, heedless of those who saw, he laughed like the lunatic he was fast becoming.

He cackled until the roar from inside the chamber grew louder. The beast was coming. The beast no one but the god of chaos controlled.

He fell into the sand laughing.

The wind sang a peaceful melody as it rushed through the cool valleys and danced around the snowcapped mountain crests. All around Anath were green meadows, bright hued flowers, and sparkling blue waters. She had seldom seen anything like it outside an oasis or around her father's hillside residence…

Anath paused as she oiled the quivers, belts, and saddles left in her care. She did not mind the mundane work because lifting her eyes she could see the cool purple and blue of the high mountains. She needed to be able to drag her mind away from the dark thoughts of the last months. Despite the calm loveliness of her surroundings the dark memories remained to haunt her with her failings and her faults.

That first night she took her bearings by the stars and set out across the flat barren landscape in the general direction of her home.

Her days in captivity had weakened her and after the fight with Hadad she had no reserves of strength. She lost her bearings and wandered into the vast emptiness of the desert. Just how long she had staggered through the heat of the day and the cool of the night she did not know. She had simply focused on moving and nothing more.

The northern traders had found her crumpled by the side of an empty watering hole. Taking her with them they headed back to their blue mountains.

Over the following days and weeks, they nursed her back to health. Friendly and quick to laugh good-naturedly she still felt alien among them with her bronzed skin and dark hair. They were all tall, fair skinned and had hair the color of flame. As she looked at them she was reminded of Dagon's wife with her red hair and flashing green eyes. Anath wondered if they were some of her step-mother's people.

They healed her body and their kindness was a salve to the deeper hurts. She sought work she might do to help her rescuers and so she cleaned the leather and gathered the wood as befitted an invalid. Her strength was returning every day and soon she would need to begin to think about what she would do. Where she should go. Did anyone live among her people? She sought her sister in her dreams but met only silence and vast emptiness.

Drawing her thoughts back she finished the last of the leather items and put them away. As she passed the storage shelves she saw the rack holding a collection of swords. Every time she passed she glanced with longing at the weapons. She had never seen finer work from any craftsman. The metal was strong yet supple and light enough that even as weak as she was they sat lightly in her hand. The blades were sharp enough to cut a hair three ways.

The traders had left several days ago and she had remained in a camp that served as a home while they traveled. She was with an assortment of older traders, women, children, and ones unable to travel easily. That meant the days were less busy than before and she had more free time.

She could not afford to allow muscles to become weak or fear to take root. This place was pleasant but eventually she had to go home. Her people might be scattered but she had duties to perform. She knew she had been wrong to leave her people defenseless against the likes of Mot's army.

Each day, while the traders were gone, she exercised with the swords. She had to regain her strength, her endurance, and, most of all, her confidence.

Selecting a small blade that she had used once before, Anath moved into a grassy clearing. Her tasks done she paused and breathed deeply of the crisp air. The sun felt good on her face and the view of the tall mountains and the tall pines made her smile.

Today her feet went naturally into the familiar steps of thrust, block, and parry. She worked hard to increase her speed. She felt the old rhythm take hold and as she moved through the steps with skill she felt a spark of life blaze deep insider her. Spinning around from a slashing move that would have felled an opponent, she halted, and instinctively raised the weapon. Several men on horseback were silently watching her.

She recognized the leader of the traders, his brother, and their gangly sons but there were others who were new to her. They all had serious looks on their faces. Another group of men waited with them. Had she broken some code of these people?

She quickly lowered the weapon, point down into the ground at her side, her grip firm on the handle. She waited for the reprimand. The trader spoke in their tongue to one of his sons and the younger man leaped off his horse. He glanced at her, with a hesitant smile, and then tugged out his own weapon.

She glanced at the old trader. "Spar." for them to spar. The younger man approached her in the wary stance of a swordsman approaching an opponent.

Instinctively, her own body moved into a counter posture. She tried to keep an eye on the group of men on horseback. With a sudden grimace and a startling bellow, designed she knew to unsettle an adversary, the young man rushed at her.

She did not attempt to block his onrush but merely stepped aside to allow his own forward movement to catch him. She spun around and struck at him with the flat of her blade. He overbalanced and tumbled to the ground. Rolling quickly he jerked back to his feet. Then he drove toward her, their swords clashed with a strident clangor, and the only other sounds were their labored breath as they lashed out repeatedly.

Each thrust was met with equal force, each step countered, and every movement instinctively known; they were equally matched. She was growing tired though; it had been too long since she had danced to a battle's tune. Her mind went back to her training at the school. *I have to best him without killing him.*

As they circled around one more time, and he raised his arm to strike a blow, she moved around sharply to his side. She aimed for the arm holding the weapon. If she could get him to raise his arm…

There was a place there… he raised his arm and she moved. *A place just there…*she nicked him and he bellowed in anger but his weapon went flying into the air.

Gasping for breath she stayed in attack stance but moved back. *Just a kiss to let you know I can do worse but choose not to,* she thought. She guardedly watched the young man as his massive chest muscles worked as he struggled to catch his breath and bright blue eyes glared at her. With a livid growl he made to move toward her but a barked command from his father halted him.

He drew in one last breath, glared at the older man, as he began clearly struggling to get himself under control. Then he nodded to her... a small smile lifted one side of his mouth as he did so. Turning away, he retrieved his sword and trotted back to his horse.

Still standing there, sword raised, she watched them all. The leader nodded, spoke in his tongue to the others, and then smiled as if something had pleased him. He led the party back toward the path. One or two of the strangers twisted on their mounts to take a last look at her.

Only as they disappeared from sight along the tree-lined path did she lower her own weapon. She placed the sword back on the rack, leaned against it, and breathed deeply of the cool air. Invigorating as the encounter had been it had also been tiring. She reviewed the last moments thoughtfully trying to discern what would greet her in the camp. Gathering her cloak, she stepped to the lake, and refreshed herself in the cool waters lapping the green grass. Somewhat refreshed, she braided her hair so it fell down her back in the fashion her mother had used, and dusted off her tunic. As she polished her boots and belt there were many thoughts spinning in her head.

The smell of fires and the smell of cooking wafted on the breeze. Only then did she head in the direction of the smell of roasting meat and the soft sounds of the music playing to entertain the guests. Whatever lay ahead, life or death, she wanted to be presentable.

As she climbed the path, the sun was setting bathing everything in a warm golden haze, and she felt her hunger rise as the aromas of many cook pots joined the scent of roasting meat.

Children darted about playing games of chase in the twilight. She saw others laughing as the young ones wove their lanky bodies between the glowing fires. No one paid any attention to her except to raise a hand in greeting or smile as she passed.

She had learned too little of their language to talk to any of them except through simple pantomime. The leader knew some of her father's tongue but few others.

She moved to the campfire near a tent with colorful tassels belonging to Amme. She was an elderly woman with a round cheerful face who wove cloth for cloaks. She had nursed Anath to health and Anath remained with her helping her as she could.

The woman loved to cook, so they had reached an agreement. Anath would help by gathering wood for the fire, helping her set up her loom, and taking care of the oxen that pulled the wagon. As a result, Anath had several new gowns and cloaks of her own. They were usually patterns the woman indicated she had been unsatisfied with for trading. They were nicer than any Anath had ever owned, though, and she appreciated them. The woman's talent with food also meant she had quickly regained her strength.

Amme stood now as she approached, a dark brown cloak trimmed by flying bird, and she threw it around Anath's shoulders. Smiling she pointed across the camp and gave her a small push.

She could see the strangers all sat with the leaders of the camp. It seemed a friendly gathering because they were all laughing and drinking. For a moment she did not move. Wariness slipped over her closer than skin. *They looked calm enough now but what might happen? Am I to die now*, she wondered. *Is there to be more fighting before this night is over?* As if sensing her momentary fright, Amme smiled, gave her another little shove, and motioned her to hurry up.

The laughter and the talk slowed and then ceased entirely as she approached the leader's fire. She took a deep breath and lifted her head high. *Remember always who you are,* she remembered that teaching and she straightening her shoulders she marched to the fire. She was her Mother's daughter, her father's child, and she would not be made small by anyone! She reached out to touch the medallion hanging from her neck and drew strength from her memories of her Mother.

At the action, one of the men murmured something in the strange tongue they spoke, and stood to come closer to her. He was tall, muscled like the traders, but his skin was honey toned in a way that reminded her of her mother. An aroma of spice, wood smoke and male animal rose as he neared and she focused on keeping her composure. Fleetingly she thought how different the scent was from the foul aroma of Mot. This man smelled of fresh air and healthy life.

His eyes were drawn to the medallion. He glanced to her, as if asking permission, and gently lifted the medallion to examine it. His eyes raised swiftly to hers then widened in almost shock. Excitedly he called something over his shoulder. Nodding to her with a flashing smile, he stepped back. He and his companions spoke for long moments.

The others at the fire eyed the encounter warily. Then the oldest one of the guests rose, his hair touched with grey over his ears, and walked over to her. He dipped his head, placed a hand inside his shirt, and pulled off a leather thong with a medallion attached. He held it out in his open hand and motioned for her to look.

She lifted the ornament from his hand into the light from the cook fires. It bore similar markings to her own. Shocked, she raised her eyes to him.

He smiled and nodded as he led her to the fireside. Sitting down, she felt hidden eyes roam over her. She knew they were examining her from her head down to the length of her legs. She ignored them all as she came back to the object in her hands. The same symbols but in different places; surely they were in the same tongue?

The older man spoke to his companions in low tones. Then he began to speak louder, not looking at her, but to the trader's chief. He spoke casually as if simply making conversation on random topics. Drink came then and everyone enjoyed the sweet wine and the warm fire. Then the leader of the strangers leaned forward to speak to the leader in their strange, melodious tongue. Finally, he sat back and nodded as he motioned for the trader to speak to the group clustered around the fire.

Frowning, the trader gathered what he had heard, and he turned to speak rapidly to one of his sons. Anath straightened up as the man spoke in her tongue.

"This man is Aqui and his people were wiped out many long seasons ago. They had to flee their homeland across the wide waters. You understand?" He made an up and down movement with his hand and she recognized the symbol for sea waves. She nodded she understood. "Good. So many perished, he says, but they know that some survived. Since he was a small boy they have been trying to find them."

The visitors turned to look at him as if they knew what he had said. She wondered if they were as ignorant of the other languages as they wanted them to think.

"They have stories and knowledge to share." The trader told her. "He asked where you found that medallion you wear."

"It was my mother's." She told him, looking directly at the old stranger. "She left it to me and a similar one to my sister."

As he repeated her answers, the strangers all began to speak to one another, and they looked excited.

"Where is she, they ask. Where is your mother?"

"She died…many years ago." She answered. She barely noticed as his son began to speak in a soft voice translating her words back into the trader language "Tell them, I have wanted to learn more of her and of her people. She died when I was a child and so could share so little about her people. I met three women some months ago who also knew these symbols. I think, if I remember correctly, they also spoke your language."

As she looked at the men around the fire, something, some instinct, stirred within her. She felt a warm presence suddenly standing, unseen but so welcome, at her side. Her voice husky and low she began to sing. It was a one her Mother had shared every night. It was important, she told them, remember it always. *The moon is shining bright across the silken seas, the dolphin leaps and the seabirds cry. Home I come before dawn's new light, before the tides new sweep, before your next sigh, before the next goodnight…*"

As she finished, the older man dropped his hand into his head and began to sob. He quickly shook off the concerned hands of those around him and spoke to them. Anath feared she had done something to offend him to cause him such grief.

He shook off his tears and speaking to the traders in short clipped sentences, he smiled. Smiling the trader translated. "He cries because his mother and grandmother sang this song. When he was a very small child. He had thought he would never hear its music again."

"I was afraid I had caused him some pain or insult."

"No, you just made an old man very happy. Come. He says to meet his sons and men."

With the trader and his son translating she at last learned all of their names. The old trader's name was Sein. The younger men his sons Mers and Tann. Tann was the one who had fought her in the pasture. He smiled now and seemed proud of his cut. The others were two of their men, Bas and Drai.

The last one was a younger son of the visitors. Mers spoke to the trader who knew some of their language. "He asks, do you know any more of these songs? He is Denie. He is a... how to say it, he is one who keeps their history, their stories, and their songs. He is their soul keeper."

"An important duty. We have such among my father's people." She nodded to the young man and launched into several songs her Mother had shared. The young man listened intently and then joined her as he mastered each one.

Then someone brought another jar of wine and they all had brimming mugs. From the depths of their packs came instruments and they demonstrated dances as merry tunes were played on strange stringed instruments.

The traders gathered around, clapping and smiling as their guests became more animated. The steps were complex and sometimes involved acrobatics as they leaped over their companions. Anath was so thrilled to find these people and, although she grieved for her lost family, she basked in the wonder of meeting her mother's people again.

Soon everyone was dancing and singing in whatever language they spoke as the fire lit the night and the wine flowed like the river lifting hearts and minds.

Over the next days, Anath learned much about her mother's people. She learned how a terrible earthquake had swallowed their island, how they had escaped in boats but the storms and waves were terrible. They had drifted for days. Many people had died and their boats had become separated. Sein shared how he had found their refugees living among a dozen people from the coldest northern lands to the deserts.

"Never in large groups", he sighed as he spoke, "but only a few here and there. Many of the young ones. They soon forgot their homes and their language."

She had learned a little over the last few days and could converse, almost childlike, without Mers or his father translating. For some questions she would need to have someone more proficient.

One day as they were talking, the others had drifted away, she made Mers swear secrecy. Then she asked the questions she had sought answers to for so long. "Ask him, how is it my sister and I know each other's thoughts? Why do our dreams have meaning? What does it mean when the medallion grows warm in my hands?"

Sein listened as Mers spoke her words. Then he simply looked at her as if he could not believe what she was saying. His look of shock needed no translation.

"He says, this is true that these things happen to you? It is no game you play?"

"No, it is all true."

Sein dropped his head and refused to look at her. "Why is he doing that? Have I done something wrong?"

The other man refused to look at her as he listened to Mer's mumbled words. Then he lifted his own face and looked at her with mingled awe and shock. He lowered his own head as he spoke to Mer.

"He says," Mer looked at her strangely but then dropped his own eyes, "there were special people among them, ones born to be our leaders, priests, and warriors. They could do these things you mention."

'That does not explain why he will not meet my eyes or why you do not either."

"These people were always mated with others like them," the man told her at last, "so the blood would run strong. Almost like gods."

A month later, walking alone across a wide dead meadow swatting away a cluster of small creatures buzzing in the air, she recalled those strange words. "If I were a god, I'd find fresh water and do away with these flying devils!"

Squinting up at the sky, she saw nothing but white sky faded by a blistering sun. In the distance, though, she saw several huge black birds circling. She judged it would take her to almost sunset to reach the spot.

The setting sun painted the sky a harsh and bilious scarlet as she found the place. The heat was like an oven and nearly overpowering was the fetid stench of the decaying bodies. Anath tied a rag around her nose and fought down the nausea.

There were almost too many of the men and animals to count. Her mind refused to accept the fact of so many sprawled in death across the plain. Gleaming ravens hopped around the bodies, their sharp beaks gouging and tearing at long tendrils of flesh. Here and there some bickered and squawked over ownership of their rancid morsels.

The harsh light from that ominous sky reflected in pools of blackened blood. Vile rivulets flowed that seemed sullen rivers linking the fallen to one another. It was a horrible liquid chain of death. The place had the feel of a nightmare come to life. Some of the bodies were stripped to bone but she saw little that told her who these people had been.

Tales told to her as a child of evil magic and monsters rose unbidden to her mind. Were there vile ghosts searching for revenge stalking through that killing field? What else could have left such horror in its wake?

A gust of hot desert wind rushed toward her and with it came a teaming mass of the black birds. Winging overhead they rushed in ever moving swirls. An endless stream of long undulating bands stretching like a shadow across the barren and death marred plain. Never had she seen so many birds in flight and the sight chilled her to the marrow.

Abruptly one band of the ravens hurried toward her so fiercely that she ducked to avoid the razor-like claws and the onslaught of ebony wings. They darted past, squawking as if angered, and then shifted upwards. They joined the vast swelling cloud of birds as they swung back over the plain. They were like a huge storm cloud as they hurried away to the dark mountains.

The place reeked of a horror worse than any she had ever seen before. Turning away in disgust she headed along the dry watercourse away from field of death.   As she walked, she kept her eyes on the horizon and remained alert for tracks of those who had caused such horror. Keeping her eyes alert she wondered if she was too late. What had happened while she had been in the land of the purple mountains and the blue lakes?

Long before she reached the camp she saw it and perched on a rocky ledge she took its measure. A small settlement but well-guarded. She noted the raised platforms and the weapons close to those who waited there. She would need to approach them carefully. Traders she had met told her that some survivors might include people who had been in her village. As she neared the entrance, she prepared to confront a wary camp, but as soon as she was seen, a loud murmur began. It rose until it sounded like a giant hive of bees unsettled by a foraging bear and then suddenly it achieved clear meaning.

"Anath! Anath! Anath!"

The chanting grew to a roar as loud as thunder. At the sound, the flap on one of the tents burst open and a woman's figure dashed out. She stared at the entrance to find the source of the mounting roar.

"Anath!" Her sister ran toward her.

"Asherah!" She saw some faces and they seemed familiar. Yes, they were from the village. They were alive! Anath ran to grasp her sister in a long fierce hug. Her little sister who still only came up to her shoulders.

As the crowd around them continued to cheer, the sisters clustered together holding each other tightly. Tears flowed down their faces as they repeated a single phrase. "You're alive!"

Finally, breaking loose Asherah ordered those around, "Go quickly and spread the word! We feast tonight! Anath, my sister, she has come home to us!"

As they crowd hurried off to prepare food and spread the news, her sister led her into the tent. As she set out pitchers of water and fresh clothes they shared what had happened to each while they had been apart. Finally, Anath asked her sister, "What is all of this?"

"What?" Her sister tilted her head. "Do you mean all the people, the camp, and those guards? An army of course."

Asherah laughed. "An army! When Mot's men attacked, Turga and others led us away to an old fort in the hills. Then, when it looked that Mot's men had carried you off, they set us after you."

"You came for me?"

"We tried. A vicious storm rose and we lost your tracks. We searched but found nothing. Finally, we had to turn back." The haunted look in her sister's eyes said more than words at what that decision had cost. "We searched for weeks and months. Then a strange beast hunted us. That was probably this creature that Mot has called up from the demon world. Winter came then trapping us here. As spring came we launched other searches but did not fare any better."

"We did not cease in wanting to find you Anath but we were not a band of warriors. Too many of us were disabled, too old and there were too many children. We did try though! We did!"

She heard the anguish in her sister's voice. "Asherah, it is alright."

"First, we sent the oldest and the youngest to the hills to hide. Then we trailed Mot but held back. He has that horrible beast at his command."

"You are right to call it a demon," she told her sister. "Or something even worse. I thought it was just some strange beast, at first, when I tracked it that night many months ago."

"You tracked it?" Asherah asked.

"It did not do me any good; the creature is wily." Anath frowned at the memory of that hunt. "It is powerful, smart, and incredibly strong as well. After seeing Mot's camp, and the monster..."

"Surely they are far enough away for some small safety now?"

"They may be closer than you know." Anath quickly shared what she had encountered crossing that dismal killing field.

"Then it is good we have been making plans. Preparing." As she glimpsed Anath's questioning look she added, "As we roamed, we gathered together others left stranded by those men. We were not the only villages they attacked. The warriors left to us have been training us to fight. Every man, woman and child able to hold a weapon. We are all willing students ready to do battle."

"Soldiers." Anath whispered recalling the people she had passed. "You said they were an army."

"Not yet, not until they have more training. They have the will and the heart. Now, what of Hadad?" Her sister asked. "Did you find him? Is he safe? I feared you were dead when the dreams were empty of you."

Hanging her head, Anath drew a deep breath. This was news she did not want to bring. She had desperately wanted a way to hide her dreams for that very reason. *How do I tell her?* Anath held out her hand to Asherah.

Asherah, sensing the change in her sister, tentatively reached out to take the hand. She had learned some things from the people she had met. A shiver rippled through Anath and reached to her sister. The younger woman's eyes opened wide. Then her hand dropped quickly. Face white, body trembling, she doubled over. Clutching her mid-section, seemed looked as if she would be sick. "Oh, God no, not that Anath! Those babies! He loved them. How could he allow that?"

"It was Mot." Anath whispered unwilling to even speak his name. "He is a truly a monster. He is a poison and draws on the most evil powers."

"None of us, not even the priestesses, understand."

"He has that terrible demon at his command." She explained about seeing the shadows around Mot. "Asherah, I have never seen anything like it before. It was fearsome. What if this power he calls is greater than we are?"

"Yes, there are foul powers are at work with this man. Everything he touches becomes dust." Asherah admitted. "It will not defeat us or our people. It cannot."

"When I touched your hand just now... a flood of images filled my head", biting her lip as tears fell down her cheeks. "I am so sorry you had to go through all of that alone. I should have known though. Why did you not dream walk?"

Anath reached out to hug her close. "The medallion was taken from me. Later, well, I did not want to burden you with...the things that were happening. I could not."

"I see. Always protecting me. Obviously you have learned skills while you were away. I will expect you to teach me. I am grown now Anath. Do see these people around her? It was I who took command."

"You, little Asherah?"

Blushing a little, she laughed. "Well, I did have some help..."

"I thought as much." Then their mirth gave way to mourning. Silently, the two mourned the loss of everything as they gripped one another tightly. Stroking her sister's hair Anath pushed her own grief away. She would save those memories for when she faced Mot and put an end to his rampages.

"Let me tell you about the men I met from our mother's people." Anath told her. "I have much to tell you about our 'gifts'."

Asherah sank to the carpets before her sister. "We have dreamed of this for so long. To learn about where she came from and who she was. More about *our* people –."

That evening Anath watched, laughing, at the group dancing around the huge fire. They celebrated the return of Anath. They were full of joy, and for just brief a heartbeat, everyone forgot the horrors of the attack the year before.

A year; Anath shook her head. Her journeys had taken her so far and she had learned much. She had known only a small sliver of the world before. Her home, though, would never be the same. Her sister had told her the childhood home on the hillside was nothing but a burned out shell. The school just a pile of rubble now nearly buried by the desert sands. The water shrinking as the evil drought seemed to rob their world of its beauty. No one wanted to go back there; all seemed to agree it was cursed.

At night, as the sun's orb sank into the horizon, Anath would often be alone on a crest of sand lost among her thoughts. After being away from larger groups of people she found that she needed time to think. So these days she often sought out the solitude.

Sitting on the hillside her sister joined her and they watched the day fade into twilight. Breaking the silence, she told the younger woman: "It is good to be with family. I am proud of you. You assumed leadership after the attack and now the people look up to you." All those lessons on leadership and planning, wasted on Hadad and even herself, had found fertile ground in their little sister.

"You have done well Asherah. Tagging along at father's heels you learned to manage people. You can plan for the future. You will be a peace keeper as well. These farmers like to bicker and you will do well at leading them."

"You are laughing at me."

"No, I remember you talking once to two shop keepers who had an ugly grudge. You convinced them to rethink their actions."

"Maybe, but I could never be like Dagon. He was a born leader. People loved him."

"You will achieve much more for them than even Dagon could." Anath looked at her sister. It was the truth. Although she had been trained in the warrior craft as well, she had always been the dreamer and many had thought she would become a priestess. "You will lead the people well and, more importantly, with honor."

"What of you? Are you going to be happy back here after all of your experiences? Can you settle down to take old Turga's place? Will you be content, here, to train the children and newcomers as fighters?"

"Good questions." She thought for a moment. "My path is not as clear. I only trained as a warrior. Since childhood to be a warrior is all I wanted. I was always happiest while hunting and later using the sword. Those are my only skills."

"If you wish you can learn to do anything."

She recalled her tasks among the trading folk in the mountains and grinned thinking of the equipment. Her mind had always been somewhere else. Thoughts of her loss and her need for action made her restless. "Outside of the sword, I have no skills and there is little else that interests me enough to learn new abilities. Only time will tell if that is wise or foolish."

Her sister laid a hand on her arm and she felt a strange warmth seep through her body. She felt refreshed in some odd way. Her sister grinned. "You do not know all there is to know...yet. Open yourself again to the dreams tonight, my sister. You will be amazed."

That night closing her eyes on her bed she recalled what her sister had said. Breathing deeply, there seemed a special perfume on the air. A fragrance rare and magical that caused her lids to flutter and a deep sleep to wash over her.

She listened as the wind passed and seemed to serenade her with a music so lovely she could weep. Arms of memory seemed to reach from the fading day to caress her with feather light touches; as if to let her know, she was not alone. She welcomed the familiar signs and knew her dreams would be of her Mother.

Dream Anath," she heard her sister whisper as if she lay beside her in the darkness. "Dream..." Flashes of soft light began to spin and with the turning of each color images blazed closer until she began dizzy and her eyes fluttered closed.

"She opened her eyes on a world so strange it made her gasp. Everything glowed in a pale dawn like light in a long, long hallway with doors stretching on into the distance. The floor glistened like silver water and on the walls were reflective decorations. She knew this place...

In the mirror like walls she saw herself, a silvery azure glow surrounding her. All around her, the glow outlined the floors and the openings in glistening sparkles of light.

She reached out to one of the openings and saw her hand disappear as if into a bucket of water. It crackled strangely, small dots of light blazing around the opening where her hand had disappeared.

Quickly, she pulled it out, but saw no harm to her flesh, and she moved on to the next opening. She noted a sword appeared at her waist as if in response to her surprise and fear.

Peering in, she jumped back suddenly as a snarling face, fierce talons, and jagged teeth filled the frame. The creature was held fast by the invisible barrier and seemed aware of the portal but not of her.

Hurrying further down the silvery hall, she looked into another opening but it seemed filled with nothing but deep night. She put her hand into the dark and felt something grip. It began tugging fiercely on her hand. She jabbed the sword into the opening and immediately something screamed a shrill protest.

Cautious now, she moved on, noting the entries she passed. Fear of becoming lost in this strange maze she began marking them in her memory.

Another opening made her cry out for a different reason. Never had she seen such vivid green and luscious foliage. Beyond was a world so filled with water she could not grasp the breadth of the rolling waves at first. Surely so much water could not be found anywhere…

There seemed a pattern to the entries as she prowled the halls. The darker the opening the more fearsome the world it accessed and the more ferocious horrors it caged.

The more luminous and open the doorway, the lovelier and more lush the worlds it overlooked. They too would challenge even the most dedicated. In their glowing sun filled worlds one could become dazed and forget duty altogether.

Always there would be the glowing ball of silver light that filled her with awareness and knowledge of this place. It fluttered by her head before it winked away and she woke; a small caressing touch as if her mother kissed her.

On and on she hurried down the hall peering into a dozen doors seeing worlds and wonders she had never imagined and haunting horrors she hoped she could forget. She knew those living nightmares must never find entry into those peaceful scenes filled with laughing families or innocent beauty.

Suddenly, her sword was back in her hand as she roamed the silver halls and she knew her task was simple. She knew her duty. She must protect the worlds from the creatures forged in hell who would seek to do nothing but destroy. She trotted down the corridors with growing confidence. This was her world. Her domain. Her responsibility...

As a student strolling with the master, she walked long shining halls, listening as her mother spoke to her trying to teach her. When the time was over, no matter where she might be in a lesson, a chiming bell sent her back to her bed. Frustrated she begged to stay. She understood so little and she feared she was a poor student. When she failed, her mother would give her a gentle look, and then begin once more.

Lying on her pallet back in the tents later, she allowed the sounds of night birds hunting and the winds dying give her special comfort. It was good to be, if not home, back among those who had made her world a home.

Over the next months, Anath set to work training the children and youth in the use of the weapons: the sword, the bow and the horse. She was one of the few who had actually experienced battle still able to sit a horse or hold the larger swords. As the days passed, her classes grew because everyone wanted to become proficient to protect their homes and be ready should they encounter Mot or his men.

At night around campfires, she shared stories of her travels or the tales told her by those in the far mountains. As a child she loved the stories told stories by Zeni and Hasai, she had enjoyed listening to the tales of the history keepers in the blue hued mountains, and now she shared those stories herself.

As soon as some became proficient enough with a weapon, she set them to working with the others and shortly she saw a training ground of skilled fighters emerge. She also found herself talking to the leaders of the various camps about what she had seen on her travels. She helped them draw maps, showed them the places of water or shade used in her journeys. She also set them to learning to speak other languages. She had learned a few words and phrases during her stay in the mountains. She had seen first-hand how useful it could be in trading. Language was a tool and she urged them all to learn as much as they could.

She helped train a troop of scouts who would help keep watch and signal with polished metal reflecting sunlight if danger approached. One day, she took a small group and set out to scout the land west of them for additional water and food. They were descending into a twisted narrow canyon when something in the distance caught her eye. On the horizon, so far away the tall purple mountains seemed a mere lump in the distance, a thin spiral of dark smoke rose into the skies.

Despite the warmth of the day she shivered in awareness. She did not have all of her sister's special talents but some she did have. She knew in her bones that the smoke was Mot's army coming back over the mountains.

She signaled to those following her and motioned a retreat. They had to get back to the camp as soon as possible. Instantly, the column of people spun around silently and began to sprint back the way they had come.

Following, she considered all she had been hearing of the army of Mot. Most agreed that Mot himself was mad spouting his death dealing god but was still the leader of lethal army. They had seen enough remains of decimated villages and caravans to support that aspect of the reports. Worse tales said the beast now roamed free to kill and, more worrisome, was no longer truly controlled by their leader.

The beast. From her dreams, she knew that in some manner the beast was part of her destiny. Just what role the monster played was far from clear. *If I killed it, would that satisfy my fate or is there something more I must do?* The dreams were still not clear! They were far too full of symbols and scenes she did not yet grasp.

On the last ridge she glanced back at the distant smoke as the last of the people moved past. Something moved in the air near her. A wave of awareness of some unseen threat. It was as real as cold water moving past her. The dark finger of smoke curled upwards as if beckoning or perhaps pointing the way to her. She had seen that odd shadowy fog before. *He was coming. How long did they have?*

She would be ready. She turned back and descended into the valley to catch up with the others. Whatever the cost, she would face him and the beast, and she had to be ready.

A few days later, Anath had confirmation of her insight on that rocky outcrop. The mood was somber in the tent. The representatives of the various family groups sat contemplating the news brought to them by the scout Daniet. The tent was filled with a sour aroma Anath recognized; the smell of fear.

"How certain are you these were the same men?" Laneth asked at last. "They could be others who are running from Mot, like all of us."

The scout stooped down and began writing in the dirt with his knife. The symbols were clear to all gathered there: the circle with the eye and the lightning bolt. It emblems carried by Mot and his army of the Death God.

"How strong are they in swords? How many horses do they bring?" One old man asked in a gruff voice. He was sitting near the back. Augist had been a warrior until his horse fell on his legs crippling him long before Anath had been born. It was like him to think in terms of strategy. "Are there women and children with them and do they fight? Do we face only armed men?"

Anath nodded at the wisdom of his questions. "From what I have seen, Mot's group does not fight with their women present. They are counted as little more than slaves."

"They are no refugees. Fifty men, with extra horses but few pack animals." The young scout told them. "My guess is that they plan to live off the land and people they plunder."

"They are delayed because of landslides in the valleys from melting snows." The other scout, Okkad, added.

"They could climb over but that would add many weeks and they would lose many horses doing that. They may be murders but they are also lazy." Daniet replied. "I think they will turn toward the tribes to the south first. They can easier raid those villages for food. Then once fortified they would head here."

Anath looked at the faces in the tent. "We do not have long to prepare to defend ourselves against this group."

"Yes." Augist agreed. "The scout is right. They will stay only long enough in the villages to restock their supplies or replace animals."

"What troubles me is the question of where is Mot? He has proved his ability as a general in battle and battles are fought by warriors. So he with this group heading west or is he hiding in the mountains?" Anath asked. "Most importantly, has he the beast with him?"

"If he has split his forces and both of them come at us we are doomed." Laneth complained. "There are not enough seasoned warriors left among us to fight his entire troop and especially if we are spread too thin!"

"We must grow then." Anath told them. "Time is short. We can sit here and wait. Try to defend an indefensible position. Or, we carry the fight to him."

"We have resources and strengths they do not have." Understanding Daniet's eyes caught hers and he stood. "The Ravens?"

"Yes," she said. "Call the Ravens to flight." The Ravens were the young men and women who had been training as warriors. They lacked experience and many had not trained long. They did have heart and the will to fight. She turned to the others. "Mot's army is made of only its men. Their way is to make slaves of their women and children. I saw this when I was a prisoner. They are considered dead weight or merely offerings for slaughter." She saw again the frail bodies of her brother's children before the fires of their God. "They see us in the same way. We are just a small group of men hindered with a large cluster of useless old men, insignificant women, and even more worthless children."

"We are different though…" murmured Asherah in sudden understanding. Quickly the others understood her meaning. Augist laughed and slapped his knee. "Very different because none of ours are useless! They are all potential fighters! We have an army to match them point for point!"

"Not only match them, old friend. Beat them." Anath shot back and then turned to rap out a command. "Daniet, send the scouts to alert the camps! Send riders to the villages to the north and the east. Tell them to prepare. The time has come to end this."

Daniet dashed out of the tent and the cry he gave was soon rising and soaring across the campfires.

"Arise Ravens! Anath's army flies!"

"Where did that come from?" Anath asked with a frown. "What is that young fool doing? It is not *my* army!"

Asherah stepped forward and laid a hand on her sister's shoulder, "It has always been your army, sister. Legend says a hero comes when the time is right. We have merely been waiting for our warrior to arrive."

"All hail Anath!" The others had stood and now cried in one voice. Anath could only stare feeling suddenly very somber. The shackles of duty settled heavily and uneasily on her shoulders. She would do what must be done and let others decide her role. She might not be the foretold hero but she would use that prophecy, if needed, to forge a powerful weapon to defeat Mot.

One hand went to the medallion hanging from her neck and, as she clasped it, there seemed to be sudden new warmth. *Are you there Mother*, she wondered, *do you signal a blessing or a warning*?

"All hail Anath!"
"All hail Anath!"

The next days were filled with preparation among the people. The riders set out before dawn to gather recruits from the clusters of people spread out along the valley floor. Anath set the others to plans for facing Mot and the beast.

"Kothar!" she called out as she saw the tall blacksmith hurrying past. "Have we enough swords and weapons?"

"Yes. We have been gathering them from every corner for months. I have had my apprentices working at the forge day and night."

"Good."

"There is one thing." The man hesitated. "Before your father had died he had me make a sword for you. It was for your birthing day celebration. The attack on the village happened and well…this is the first opportunity I have had to speak with you."

The man went over to his wagon and pulled out a bundle wrapped in leather. He held it out to her.

"My father ordered this made…for me?"

"Yes. He gave me very specific instructions. He said you would understand them. He was very proud of his warrior daughter."

She pulled apart the leather of the bundle and her eyes widen as the sun reflected off the most beautiful sword she had ever seen. It surface was like a mirror and its brilliance nearly blinded her. She raised it up and slashed down swiftly feelings both its solid weight and its balance in her hand. Incised symbols appeared and she twisted the blade around. They were the same as found on the small box left to her by her mother. The language of her mother's people she knew now.

On the other side were symbols of her father's people, of Dagon's people. She ran a hand over the symbols marveling that her father would have such a weapon made for her. He had been so silent she had often wondered if he cared for her at all. He had ordered her a fine bow and now this. He had been a strange and complex man indeed.

"He said these were the marks of your Mother's people and you would appreciate that."

She would not cry in front of the man, but she felt like it, as she lifted the sword. "Yes, they are words in her tongue. It is a thing of beauty, Kothar. The finest weapon I have ever seen."

"As I made it…" Kothar paused as if debating what he was saying. "As I worked the metal, and stoked the flames, it felt as if it were not just my work. I felt the presence of others guiding my arm as I worked the metal. Maybe the legends are true and our ancestors do help in times of need."

"I hope so, Kothar. I hope so."

Sooner than she had imaged the group was ready. Anath jumped to the back of a shaggy mud colored horse and took a long look around her. The people were not the leanly muscled battle swords of Mot's men. Those waiting for her orders included men whose heads were as bare as a newborn. Youth, boys and girls, not too long from their own cradles. Old mothers and young men stood shoulder to shoulder. All of them waited for her command with eerily similar gazes of trust and determination.

She wondered for a moment if she was right to lead them at all. How could she lead them to what would be, for some of them, their sure deaths? How could she live with herself for causing the deaths of so many people?

Raking her eyes over the group again, though, she saw them differently. She people who had survived and were now committed to victory. She saw people who had suffered great pain and knew they fought to save others from such heartache. Each face, young and old, was etched with a sense of justice and a will to set their world right once more.

She recognized they were also similar to those who followed Mot. Perhaps more than she had ever noticed until this moment. After months of practice and training everyone was a skilled warrior and committed to one purpose.

Revenge, the wise ones said, was a bitter poison that would flow back on those who sought its sweet taste. Justice, however, was sweet and that was what they sought now. She prayed the great goddess and the good gods would favor their efforts with success.

Now, many hours later, all around her the raucous sounds of battled raged as people joined in a wild dance of struggle and swift death. Anath knew that each battle held bitter dregs. Victory could be an elusive prize.

Anath and Asherah fought side by side. Sometimes it seemed as if they fought as one being. Instinctively, they seemed to know how the other would respond, and acted before the moment came.

They had successfully tracked a group of Mot's men as they had sought water. They had attacked the raiders before they even knew they were near. Even as part of the army turned to face their party, however, a couple had raced off across the plain to warn Mot.

Now, as the battle slowed, Anath lifted herself up to look around. Uncertain of what she might see, she breathed a thankful sigh as saw most of the ones left standing were all her people. Breathing deeply, she lifted her head to allow the tiny fingers of breeze to briefly cool her blood spattered skin.

She looked at Asherah who nodded she was well. To the others she ordered: "Gather what supplies and weapons they carried. Fill the water bags."

"We ride?" One of the women asked as she gathered her spent arrows.

Anath focused on the horizon where she knew Mot waited. "We ride!"

A day later, they had slowed trying to find the trail of the other party on the rocky ground. The winds had been too strong and nothing remained of their tracks.

"We are too many." Anath remarked. They rested after another exhausting, but fruitless, search for any trace of the mercenaries.

"You think we should break apart?" her sister asked.

"We can cover more ground that way."

"Yes. That is true. Will it make us too vulnerable, though, if we encounter Mot's men?"

"We could have a hundred more and as long as Mot has that beast to command, it would not be enough. Our best strategy is to keep pressing at them and allow no chance for them to rest."

"Yes, you are right." Her sister stood. She used an arrow and drew in the dirt. "We are here, or at least I believe, we are close to this location. I will lead a party southward and return to the west. If you go northward and return to the east we should meet at the rocky pool between. That way we will have covered a great area."

"It is a good plan. Be careful sister, those rocks can also provide good cover for the enemy."

"I will be careful. Do not worry about us. Take care for yourself and do not die!"

Two days later, Anath waited with growing impatience. Her sister's group should have met them at the rocky pool by now. A growing tension seethed through the fighters at the delay. Each new gust of wind drew eyes toward the direction Asherah's party should arrive. When the wind settled, however, there was nothing but empty plain and silent horizons.

At sunset, after a day with no sign of her sister or her group, Anath gathered her weapons. She ordered everyone to prepare to head toward the south.

"In the dark?" some questioned.

"If there has been trouble, the sooner we get to them the better. Besides, it will be cooler in the dark. Weren't you complaining of the heat just yesterday?"

Cautiously they followed the narrow paths through the rocks. Just after the dawn, as the sun was high and hot in the sky, one of the scouts hurried to her. "I found something Anath!"

Anath, pulled her mount to a stop as the man rode to her.

"Back there, I found tracks of some of our horses. A few footprints as well surrounded by many horses. It looks like they herded them away into the hills. If I remember this area, where they went there is water and cover."

"Then they might still be alive." Anath looked toward the rock-strewn hills in the distance. She focused on those distant hills remembering what she could about their terrain. On the side closest to them, there were tall and jagged rock walls too steep for animals to climb. Mot's men would have moved around the base to access the easier animal trails on the far side. Even if they headed up the far canyons, they would still use those easier paths.

"Move into the foothills!" she slid from her horse and handed the reins to one of the young women standing nearby. "We will have to leave the horses here. We can be faster and quieter if we reach them on foot."

She sought out two of the warriors. "Move the people around to the far edge of the hillock." She pulled together her water bag and her weapons. Quickly she directed the others: "Set someone to tending the horses and supplies. Keep the horses together and well watered. We may have to leave quickly."

Briskly, Anath and a small group, moved out across the sand toward the rock face. Up close it looked insurmountable. Anath swung her sword over her back and jumped up to grasp a small open crevice. Swinging outward, she found a place for one sandaled foot to rest. Except for the occasional clatter of pebbles, or the grunt from exertion, they climbed upwards silently. The climb was hard and precarious in places.

Moving as swiftly, and as noiselessly, as possible, they scurried over the last of the rocks at the summit. As they hauled the final fighters over the top, they took a wary look around, and Anath noted a small overhang nearby. That might be useful if they had to hide. Stealthily, scouts moved out in several directions to study their location.

One of the forward scouts, Tes'm, who had followed a path leading upward, returned and quickly held up a hand for silence. Gesturing, he called for the other scouts and Anath to join him. As they neared, he gestured again for caution, and then disappeared into the foliage around them. The others sought cover as well.

No one moved.

Anath strained to hear what the man had noticed. At first all she could hear was the beating of her heart. Then she heard it, very faint, and recognized it as the rattle of horse's hooves on exposed stone.

Inching forward, noiseless and crouched low, she joined the scout. He whispered, "There is a cave below. They appear to have moved the captives into it out of the sun."

"Can you tell how many men?"

"There are only a few with the horses. It is a guess how many may be in the cave with the others."

She looked at the Tes'm. "Pick two or three who are stealthy. Backtrack a bit and then climb down the rocks into that opening we passed. Be ready to take them by surprise then. We will join you and then take the cave."

Purple shadows were just crawling across the floor of the canyon when Tes'm crept forward with his party. They were like the shadows themselves, silent and invisible to Mot's men. In moments, Tes'm was poised at the entrance of the cave and as Anath joined him, they slipped silently into the depths of the cavern.

It was dark and they clung to the shadows as they entered but there was a familiar foul odor to the cave. Anath paused; was the beast with them? There was no obvious trace of the monster, so it was more likely the rank smell of unwashed bodies and old rotted meat bones.

Slinking down the cave they quickly overpowered one man and then they pushed forward into the shadows. At a rocky outcroppings further inside the depths of the cavern, the halted. Anath peered into the larger chamber. The prisoners were there and she relaxed as she saw her sister alive. She raised her hand and said, "Now!"

Her warriors spilled out into the chamber. The villagers moved with a keen efficacy and deadly result. Anath cut her sister free and handed her a knife to free the others. Mot's men struggled but were soon overcome in the cramped space

"Wait!" she called, as they seemed set on killing them all. "We must find where Mot and his beast hide."

One of the villagers hauled one of the raiders to here ordering him to speak. "They left through the opening there."

"Take the others back. I will take only a few to end this. "Anath directed them. "Gather all the supplies and weapons."

Instinct alone seemed to guide her they followed after Mot. There was only a narrow channel cut through the rock by the feet of countless animals seeking water. Then the rock face gave way to earth and soon they found a track in the sand. To Anath, the trail blazed with the same silver glow from her dreams. She followed it confidently. If she survived, and only then, she would puzzle how that might have come about.

The sight of that misshapen track made every one of them grip their weapons closer. Nervously everyone looked around searching for some sign they were watched. Finding the trail of the beast controlled by Mot was a surprise. She did not like surprises and suspected a trap. Is he with the monster, Anath wondered, hiding in the shadows?

"Will we follow it?" Her sister had moved to her side.

The trail led off into the distance and around it were the faint traces of a few men and horses. "Where the monster is there we will find Mot. We follow the tracks."

Chapter 20

In the great sagas and epic tales, heroes met their nemesis with sage or witty words and bravado courage. How often, Anath wondered, did they unexpectedly stumble on each other as a crippled horse struggled to rise and opposing warriors looked on in utter surprise at the encounter?

Following the tracks across the sands, the small band of warriors had made good time. They felt certain Mot had sought to rejoin his men. He had pushed forward to gain the distance necessary to lose his trackers. A howling wind sprang up masking all sound and raising brown clouds of course dust. "An incantation?" Asherah muttered wrapping a cloth around her face. "It is hard to get and keep our bearings"

"We must keep going...no matter what." Anath told, hoping they really were headed in the right direction as they spotted an outcrop of rocks ahead.

As they rounded a turning in a canyon, however, the scene before them might have been humorous under different circumstances.

Mot stood with a few others by a sleek black horse whose foreleg was viciously broken in a hole. The animal whipped his head around, his eyes wide and panic stricken, as it struggled to rise but could not. The wind's shriek hid the animal's shrill cries of agony.

For what seemed a lifetime, but was mere seconds, the two groups stared at one another. With harsh shrieks, Mot's men' lifted weapons and lunged at the newcomers.

Anath leaped off her horse, followed by her warriors. Every blow found its target with deadly accuracy. Again she felt the strange warmth seep from the blade into her body. No, she realized with a start, her warmth filled the sword as if her life were feeding into the metal. Whatever the cause, as she plowed into the midst of the savages, a swathe of bodies lay in her wake.

A fire flickered inside of her stoking the flames of retribution. Blade singing she set her sights on Mot. It would end here and now.

She drew him away like a bull for the slaughter. He came striding to her and she looked him the eyes. They were dark pits holding nothing but shadows. She hoped that when he looked in hers he saw his death.

With a cry she raised her sword. Their blades met and sparks erupted from the force of the impact.

She advanced, she retreated, and she spun from his blows to deliver her own. All around the winds sang a wailing lament and howled with brutal intensity.

It was a brutal yet strangely elegant dance of death. She felt her senses heightened to an extraordinary level never before experienced. The sword spun in her hand with a strange warmth as she countered his every powerful move.

The long hours of practice made her able to stand against each impact of his blows. The long hours imprisoned made her able to withstand his thrusts. The memory of her loss made her incapable of failure. She noted he had to retreat more than once from her own assault.

She tightened her grip on the sword as she launched herself at the man.

No give.

No pause.

No mercy.

There was just her steady forward movement with each deadly blow. She forced him back until, in desperation, he pushed at her seeking to take back some space.

She could not allow that.

Blow met blow in steady rhythm. The sound as blade-met-blade was a strange hypnotic melody of deadly throbbing music.

Gulping air, sweat glistened, and beginning to make mistakes Mot struggled against her. The tension in air grew as he realized she would not give up. Her muscles burned but she knew she had to end this here and now.

A thousand lessons ran through her mind as she sought for some memory that might aid her now. Tensely she called out, *Mother, if ever I needed your help, it is now!* Something, like a dash of frigid water, flowed into her bones.

I am always with you my daughter. Isn skilh mo cjok milkon 'tah. She was herself but she was not alone and she moved to grip the sword differently and with new confidence. *Thank you mother.* She raised her head and smiled at Mot.

"Enough!" Her voice was thunder. She moved instinctively into the steps. She spun around abruptly sending him off guard. Just a fraction of a moment but it was enough. He raised his sword arm to block her but she was already moving in close. Her blade slashed deeply into his side. With another spin, she jerked the blade around and plunged it savagely into his exposed abdomen.

Eye to eye they stared at each other. He gripped at her, clawing at her and trying to stand. She braced herself to hold him on solid edge of the sword. Sudden fear flared in his face as he looked at Anath. As his eyes lost their focus, she felt the other presence slide away from her. She was once more just herself. He slid to his knees still clutching at her.

She thought of her family.

She thought of her friends.

She thought of all the people in countless homes. All that he had destroyed as he venerated his malevolent god of death.

She felt so tired. So much death.

The wise ones said revenge and justice were two sides of the same cup. Had she become what she hated and hunted or had she simply done what was right? Her father had said vengeance was bitter. She realized that justice might be needed but could also be bittersweet.

His sword clattered to the ground. "Justice. You should have listened." Anath gasped into his face. "You should have learned."

She ran the blade of her sword swiftly across his exposed throat. A ribbon of red cascaded from his mangled throat and down his front still clutching at her.

"I warned you what would happen when next we met. You should have listened."

He looked at her with eyes already dead and then toppled over into the dirt of the canyon floor.

Only then did she relax, she stepped back away from his form and speared her sword point in the dirt. For a moment, it was all that held her up, she drank in long, deep breaths. She willed her muscles to hold her upright just a little bit longer.

The sound of pounding feet moved her and she grabbed the sword to twist around to face the canyon. Several men burst through the opening. They skidded to a stop and looked at the body at her feet and at her as she raised the blade.

Shakily, gripping the sword hilt with aching hands, she assumed a stance to fight.

Can I handle them all? She took in the bulk of their thighs and arms. *If these giants rushed me, could I fight them when I am this exhausted?*

"Sister!" Suddenly Asherah was pushing through the wall of hulking men; a sleek unafraid hound amid lions. "You are alive!"

Her sister ran to her with enough force she nearly fell. She laughed. It was feeble but it was a laugh. It felt strangely good. How long had it been since she had really laughed at anything?

She gave her sister a hug in return. She realized then that the winds had died and the sky had cleared. "Did you think I would let the likes of him kill me, sister?"

"Such bravery?" Her sister mocked.

"I thought you were back with the villagers headed to safety."

"How could I leave you when there were reinforcements?"

Anath nodded at the men. "Your friends?"

"These are some of Kasem's men from the northern tribes. Mot's army destroyed their villages."

One the men came to where the women stood. Anath had seldom seen men so tall. She had to bend her neck back to look him in the eye.

"I am Adad. We decided to find Dagon but learned he was dead and the village scattered. So we rode to join any warriors standing against Mot." The man's voice was so deep it rumbled like approaching thunder. His eyes took in the body on the ground. He grinned suddenly, "Looks like we have found them"

"Then we are allies and friends." Anath told him.

Long hours later, the dark sky arching overhead, Anath sat at the fire. The blaze was small but its bright warmth was comforting. She lifted a piece of meat gingerly away from the flame and handed it to her sister. She gobbled it down, like a child, careless of the grease dripping down her chin. Anath sat her own piece of meat aside to cool.

It would be just as good cold. Her time in the camps had taught her anything not maggot infested was a feast and right now her food was peace.

Anything which did not kill her could be used to live another day. Maybe even a day or two beyond that.

She had set guards in case the rest of Mot's army attacked but she suspected, without him, they had no desire to attack a larger force. They would no doubt turn on each other as they fought for control within their own ranks. If lucky, they would do away with each other without bothering the valley anymore.

What worried her was the beast. Despite their searches, from the foothills to the edges of the deep desert, they had found no sign of the demon creature. That troubled her, because there was no assurance a creature of such mystery would act as one hoped. How to find it though?

"Anath, I have been thinking, and I think I know what we must do. At least a part of what we must do."

She turned to see her sister's head inches from her own. "Go on, tell me what should come next."

"Walking with our mother in dreams has taught me many things. It has shown me also that there is so much I do not understand. Sometimes it even seems she is fading away from us."

Anath nodded. She had seen the same thing. She also knew the frustration in seeking answers in such encounters. She waited for her sister to tell what she had seen.

"You know there are other places? "She queried. "Some like it is here and others very different."

"Yes, I have seen this. The many doors in that place." The memory of those strange doors in the dream hallway was clear. "I always felt that they were important. I felt certain that if I had entered one I might never have returned."

"Exactly! She says the creature, this demon, is from one of those places. It cannot be killed here. Not in our world. It is a thing of spirit and of forces we do not know."

"Then how?"

"There is so much to learn and so little time! I want to try the ritual she shared. It may seal away the beast for a time, if I have understood the dream correctly, and that will give us opportunity to learn more." Her sister pulled a hand through her curly hair, her face filled with worry. "*If* I have understood anything about this ritual correctly, it may work. It be, I fear, a great gamble."

"All of life is a wager. If there is any way to halt that monster, we must try it. Toss the dice sister." Anath laid a comforting hand on the girl's shoulder. "We have to do what we can to protect our people."

"Let me dream again tonight and then tomorrow we will do this."

"Alright. There is a sheltered spot just beyond the campfires. There is an outcrop of rocks and the caves just beyond. That seems a good place to do this." Anath told her. "We will meet there at dawn.

The next morning, just before the first tiny flickers of dawn pushed back at the shadows, Asherah joined her at the rocks. Kneeling in the sand, she took the sword given to Anath and the medallion left by their mother and arranged them in front of her. Straightening her shoulders, she raised her head and began. They stumbled through the words of the ritual. Asherah poured oil and water on the ground. Something in the shadows howled in pain. Asherah and Anath, spoke the words they had learned, and poured out the rest of the water and oil on the ground.

"Hilka! Hilka!" At their feet the water dampened soil simmered, bubbling like a pot on the fires, and a new series of howls screamed through the dawn. The horses whinnied and shuffled nervously. Anath could see that a few in the camp grabbed weapons and looked worriedly around them.

"If I have done it right - , "Asherah muttered. "Then that should slow the beast down. Maybe enough to catch up. It is now trapped in that form for a time."

"Will it be enough to force it back into the caves?"

"I cannot say with certainty. Mot called up this fiend from some place I cannot even name. Who knows what it can do? He thought he controlled it but look at the truth of that claim. Apparently, such beings are tricky."

"They can soon master those who seek to control its power." Anath nodded. "It certainly turned on Mot."

"While it was linked to Mot, the being could be sent over vast distances like a wisp of vapor. All the while the other one linked to it could feel and see all it did."

"Do we have a chance to destroy the beast?"

"No. We cannot destroy it. Binding it and locking it away are the best we can do. For now."

"Locking it away inside one of those dream doors."

"Yes. I still do not have all the answers. The link to mother is so much weaker for some reason."

"Yes, when she speaks now it is often in her own language." Anath nodded, remembering her own experiences.

"Part of this plan is from what she said and my own guesswork."

"Well, we will make it enough." Anath promised. "Sometimes, outside of the dreams, I feel a connection to mother. That might help us."

"Why cannot she be plainer to us? Some things are clear and easy to grasp but other lessons are harder to understand."

"I know. It is frustrating."

"What are we saying?" Asherah grunted in an exasperated tone. "Listen to us! We visit with our dead mother in our dreams and then complain. We are not children!"

"No, we are not and we will do this. So, the binding ritual should draw the creature to us. Then we can return it to its own place. Tell me sister," Anath asked, "Once we drive it into that place, just how long will it be bound?"

The peaceful stillness was shattered in an instant as the beast, roaring, burst into their midst. Frightened men and women went scrambling to reach swords. Shrill screams said not all had been swift enough to escape the creature's bloodlust.

How had it crept up on them? Anath jumped up grabbing her sword and hurried to the sounds of the screams and growls. *Had the thing waited in the dark, watching, till they were at their most unwary?* The idea that the beast might have the cunning and intelligence of Mot was more horrifying than the sheer bestiality of the creature.

A hoarse cry rent the predawn as one of the swords slashed into his thick hide. He sprang up, bounding past them and rushing into the night.

Without a thought Anath hefted her sword and hurried after the creature. In the bright moonlight the trail was clear and she hurried to follow it. It seemed to limp and she pressed forward sure it must be wounded and an easy target.

A long time later, however, she paused to find herself separated from the others and on her own. Hearing a twig snap behind her, and sensing something was in the night with her, she realized she was in trouble.

She had underestimated the creature and such mistakes could kill. She had been careless in allowing it to trick her like that. Was she a feeble old man or a silly child to let the creature turn her, a warrior of so many battles, into the hunted?

She gripped the hilt of her sword. Her old teacher would have had her lashed for such a careless hunt.

She stared toward the horizon where the brute had left a trail in the high grasses. Seeing that she knew what she had to do.

Part of the ritual they had used worked. They had trapped the beast into a solid form.

The only sound now was the whisper of the wind. It ran through the withered old fingers of nearby bushes with a slight rustle. Straining harder, she could barely pick up the faint murmur of the river some distance to the south. It ran from the mountains and then spilled across the desert wastes. It would make an easy route to avoid detection.

The beast had grown as still and as quiet as death itself. Its false trail leading out into the open was clever...too clever. She chided herself for briefly thinking that perhaps the creature had been more badly wounded than she had first realized.

No, it was still out there. With every fiber of her being she was certain of that. She was now the hunted ...

What was that?

Every muscle tensed as she raised her sword and spun around. The thing attacked.

Wielding the blade with as much strength as she could gather, she slashed, and jabbed the beast.

Even trapped in a solid form, it still made a difficult target. Her blows reverberated as if hitting stone. Her hand ached from the grip on the sword. Gritting her teeth at the sudden pain, she brought the sword around thrusting into the soft underbelly of the creature. It roared, raising its head, to scream into the night and then charged toward her.

Stumbling, she caught herself, but the creature lashed out with claws sharper than any eagle's. It lunged forward toward her and she raised an arm to protect herself and felt the thing slash deep into her flesh...

A pain shot into her head as a voice said, *"Stop chasing the beast now and let him follow you. Now is the time to lead him to the dream. Only there can he be contained."*

She recognized the voice of her sister but the face arising in her mind was of her mother.

She knew where to go now. She raced ahead, shouting and calling into the night. She taunted him with her words and her dash into the open. Inviting the creature to follow her made herself visible as she pushed into the darkness. Behind her she heard a fearsome growl and a howl that gave her chills. A foul musky scent eddied out in tendrils as if to pull her down. It was behind her now. She could hear its rasping breath as it began to chase after her.

Across the open grasses she sped feeling the creature running behind her. Climbing the rocky path she paused at the entrance to the cave. Flinging a look over her shoulder, she saw the misshapen creature still hurtling after her. It was close enough that a stinking stench moved ahead of it. The smell was like a wave of filth and made her suddenly feel sick. Just a few more yards.

In the cave opening ahead she saw her sister already there. Asherah urged her to hurry as she speared a torch into the ground. Its flickering light made shadows dance in the night wind. Behind her, ghostlike, faces of people flickered in the gloom briefly.

The guttural bellow was closer now and she raced to the cave. It roared as it loped after her. A hollow, malevolent sound that thundered around them.

The creature's hot breath blasted her and doubled her pace as she mounted the last length of the trail. A vicious claw ripped out and snagged her tunic. She nearly stumbled but swerved to avoid the other claw.

Dashing on she leaped upwards to catch the jutting ledge and hauled herself over onto the plateau. Grasping the medallion around her neck, afraid now to even look behind, she sprinted into the aperture to the cave. It gaping maw sat waiting like eager ravenous jaws.

Give me strength, and courage, Mother, she thought, *give me strength!*

Once inside the opening a light, as bright as the sun, exploded all around them.

Chapter 21

"Hurry!" Asherah came running in from the darkness. She merely glanced as she brushed past the creature frozen in place. "Hurry!" she called.

"How did you do that?" Anath asked.

Nearly dragging Anath further into the cave, Asherah urged: "Later! We have no time to lose. Gather round now!"

Others from in from the dark of the cave to join them in the pale light. Anath recognized them as some of those training to be Priests. They looked frightened but hurried to take their places near the pack were Asherah had placed the swords, the medallions, and more.

"How did you get these back?"

"Later! We have so little time! Stand there." Asherah took her place and Anath took hers. "I promise to answer everything but not now!"

As she spoke, Asherah arranged the items before her. There was urgency to her movements that communicated to all of them. "We must hurry!"

She stood suddenly pouring a substance on the ground; the liquid bubbled and hissed in a strange burst of smoke. Lifting up the medallion she cried out: "*Ishk Medoch sunum persh. Hilka!*

A cold wind whirled around them like a serpent coiling and tightening.

"Hilka! Hilka!"

The words came stronger and with more confidence this time. Then, like a chorus, the young men and women of the Priests joined their voices.

The air twisted around them flexed and warped to fit some new form. Spikes shimmered like lightening and the ground beneath distorted and heaved resisting the powerful insistence of the words.

"Hilka! Hilka!" Their voices mingled as one thunderous chorus. With a growl the beast awoke and surged over the crest of the ledge. If a nightmare could fly that would the image as it landed in their midst. Its massive arms sent people flying and the sounds of the chanting changed to cries of pain. Its horrific claws lashed out as its bellow made them deaf. Then it was just a blurring motion lashing out. A mindless creature of death and repulsion.

Anath dragged her sword up. Asherah lay still where she had been tossed aside by one of the blows. Even as she noted this, though, she saw Asherah leaping to her feet. A wet ribbon of blood dripping down her face and her look one that glowed with fierce authority.

In fact she glowed in truth. A vivid blue light surrounded her as she thrust out one hand as if to grasp the beast, and held high the medallion.

"Hilka! Hilka!" Her voice roared as powerfully as the beast. The cave walls rang with the awful power of the words. The walls cried out in echo of the words. The beast shook its shaggy head and snarled at them.

The others, struggling up or still on the ground, joined their voices to the ritual. The sound was a hammer blow filling the cave. The sound reverberating in the bone. It was thunder shaking the ground.

"*Hilka! Ashkim, mehr Anath!*" Asherah stabbed the sword into the ground. A profound rumble shook the earth deep beneath them.

"*Yey besh birkin sahm 'El gezir! Be gone by the power of the words! Settle down into darkness...*"

As the words began, the air around them began to sizzle and the air seemed to grow thin. The very air burst into blue flame and turned to ash and before fluttering around like a flock of birds. Each breath was a labored struggle.

"Hilka! Hilka! Deep into the dark you must go!"

Relief at seeing her sister was alive was followed quickly by concern as another sound rippled upwards from the dark heart of the cave.

In that darkness, she could see a faint blue light burst into life. It burned with light so bright she thought it might burn her eyes, yet still she stared because it called to her. She knew that light and she knew what it meant.

Long, dense curling fingers of light shot out from the very rock of the cave and tangled themselves around the beast. Deep inside the cave a blackness grew that was darker than any night. Yet at its heart was a pulsing luminosity.

Like chains of smoke, the fingers of light pulled the thing back into the dark opening and toward that light. The swirling ashen shards were drawn to it as well. The creature, as if sensing his doom snarled, dug his heels into the ground. As he struggled deep channels were cut into the dirt as he tried to resist.

Words spilled out of her then but she did not where they came from: "Traveler of worlds you must return!"

The ground shuddered convulsively then, and with a hideous screaming roar, the creature was dragged into the light blinding cavity of the cave. It struggled, claws scoring the earth, trying to escape that hideous and awesome light.

A glacial wind stirred, for brief moments, within the airless space. Unseen fingers tugged at her hair and she felt she could have reached out and touched some being. Then it too went hurtling on into that darkness. She moved, almost instinctively to follow after it, but felt a grip on her arm and stopped.

That light. It pulled at her refusing to be denied. She knew that strange glowing blue light and she knew it sparkled like liquid metal. It was almost a yearning...

"Anath! No, you can't follow him." Her sister tugged her back.

"I have to! I do not understand it myself; I just know that *this* is my destiny and my purpose." Despite the pain she felt in a dozen aching muscles and the weariness, she knew she had to follow that creature and that light. No matter how far, or how hard the journey, she just knew she was part of that light.

A throaty roar down the belly of the dark cavern sent shivers. She could hear the murmurs of fear from the group still frozen in place near the entrance.

"What is that creature?" One of the young Priests whispered. Her face was pale; they were all children in that moment and once more afraid of the dark and the sounds that filled its emptiness.

"Mot's demon." Anath breathed deeply looking around.

"I think it is also something more." Said one of the Priests. He was a young man not yet old enough to have a beard. His voice was firm as he spoke. "It is ancient beyond measure and not really of this world."

Asherah nodded, "In truth, maybe there is no word for it in this world. At least, none we know." Another growl reverberated through the cave.

Anath felt again the insistent urge to move further into the cave. The sound had been different though. It had been muffled and angry. Suddenly she saw where it waited held by the blue light. She did not need to explore the deepest crevices of the caverns she knew them already. They were familiar to her from a dozen long dream walks with her mother. This was the place of her dreams.

The doors were gateways to other worlds. She did not understand all that meant but the words filled her head and with them came some small measure of understanding.

"It is locked away in that...place. For now. I cannot say for how long." Asherah told her as she collapsed onto the floor of the cavern. Her sister's eyes closed and rivulets of sweat stripped her face. "I do not know if it will hold forever. It will hold perhaps long enough to learn more. Till we gather our own forces."

"Even small mercies can make all the difference." Anath said. "You did much in a short time."

"It was not easy. We may need other items for the ritual. Things I did not recognize from the vision. There is so much to learn! I would need to live a thousand lives to master it all."

"It is locked away for now," Anath mused," but is it trapped?"

"I do not know. It may hold through a lifetime or fail tomorrow."

Anath crouched down beside her sister. Her eyes kept going to the entrance to the deeper cavern where the light pulsed. To where the light *called*...

Some force tugged at her and she felt a need to walk into those depths. She would walk those shining halls. With the thought she realized the decision had been made. If, that was, it had ever been hers to choose. What chain of events had set this moment into her future? Had it been decided from before Hasai found her mother wondering in the desert? Dragging her thoughts away she tried to lighten the mood. "Then, sister, you will have to marry and have many fat babies to teach it all too!"

"I may marry or I may not; I have not decided. Give me your hand."

She laid her hand in her sister's warm clasp. Asherah held it tightly for a moment and closed her eyes. She ran her palm over the back of each of their hands murmuring something. It reminded Anath of a lullaby from childhood. Her sister's voice was too low to understand the words.

Anath waited, she shivered under a sensation as if warm oil flowed over her head, to ripple down her body enveloping her in its rich embrace. The sensation astonished her but seemed to invigorate her as well. She seemed to be so much more aware of her surroundings, invigorated, and renewed.

She felt a strange peace. "Thank you." Anath whispered, accepting the strange gift. Her sister had talents both strange and wonderful. Asherah, her eyes closed and her head thrown back, still gripped her hand. She glowed with that bright nimbus of crackling light.

"Yes, I see it now, sister. That place flashes with the strange and terrible. It shifts and spins sending out sparks in the dark sky." Asherah warned, "There are many worlds there. Many dangers. It is a place of waiting where time has no meaning."

Her sister's slim hand reached out to touch her temple, and when she did, they both gasped. She was sucked into a whirlpool of light and sound. Anath felt herself spinning and her own eyes closed tight to steady herself.

Had her sister found a way to enter the dreaming vision while still awake? Her strength as a seer was apparently growing stronger and faster than she could have ever imagined.

Asherah's eyes shot wide open.

"You are *she who walks between the worlds*! You are the one."

The words uttered by the old trader Hasai so many years ago when he had first seen their Mother. Later, when she was a child he had claimed his vision had been about Anath. Most had taken it for the babbling of a senile old man.

What chain of events had set this moment? She had not wanted to admit that everything she learned about her mother made it clearer. This strange legacy tied her to a heritage she could not yet fathom.

A thunderous shot rumbled from the deepest belly of the caverns followed by a pounding roar. The light, that blinding glow, flickered. Clearly then, in her mind, she saw the source of the disturbance. She jumped to her feet.

One of the enclosures in that strange corridor was heaving in and out as if it breathed. More pounding erupted. It was stronger this time and caused splinters of wood to burst from the casement holding the heavy closure. The light flickered again as if under assault by strong winds that would see darkness consume its flame.

"The Guardian...She Who Walks Between the Worlds...must be fearless." She heard the soft voice of her Mother. *"She must be a force of justice and mercy. In other worlds, there are creatures of magnificence and goodness beyond imagining. There are also, in some worlds, beings whose brutality is a thing of endless nightmares."*

In her mind, she could see clearly that door as it bulged under the impact of the next blow.

"The beast must be taught to obey and accept its banishment to its world. You use the words to make them retreat. Every world knows these words and responds. Using the ritual the weak barrier is made secure once more."

With her mother dead, there had been no one walking between the worlds, and this had allowed Mot's creature to escape. She understood now. Without a Guardian in place, *"She Who Walks Between the Worlds"*, the clever monster had used Mot to bring it out of that abode. Used him to begin a bloody rampage.

All around them the cave sparkled to life just like the one in her dreams. Glowing lines and throbbing colors painted the stone halls. A gateway bloomed to life and its light throbbed in invitation.

Across the door were the same writings she had seen earlier and the incisions burned with a vivid amethyst blaze. As they pulsed across the symbols like lightening across a tempestuous sky she recognized them as her mother's language.

"I must go for a time." Anath hefted her sword from its sheath. Briefly she saw her face reflected in the blade. "Be safe my sister. I will depend on you to find the ritual that will forever banish the creature and guard those worlds we saw. I will talk to you in dreams."

Trotting down the passage, the sword in her hand, she rehearsed the words of command, "Hilkah, Hilkah..."

At the doorway, the sword in her hand grew warm. The symbols glowed and lights flashed in the metal. The entryway became clear showing her the creatures crowded around the gateway.

Raising the blade up, she cried out the command. "Hilkah!" The blade flashed and passed through the doorway carrying her with it into the scene of madness.

Screeching and growling there were creatures all backing away from the glowing sword. Some nervously backed away, some were running in fright, but all responded to the sight of the sword. Guided still by this strange new instinct she pointed the sword toward them and they retreated. Doors slammed shut and the sound of locks falling into place followed. Sheathing the now quiescent sword back into the scabbard on her back, she turned to survey where she was. These corridors that were now her domain and her world.

There were so many more of them to explore. There was a growing excitement and curiosity building inside her.

Her sister would do all she could to find the binding that would serve to guard the worlds from the sinister intrusions of man and creature alike. Until that day came, she knew who she was and accepted it, feeling suddenly and completely at peace.

Soon the hallway was clear and quiet.

Behind her the clear doorway clouded until she saw nothing but an ordinary stone door barring entrance. Her old life was truly gone.

She Who Walks Between the Worlds headed further into the dark passage ahead. She knew she had a destiny filled with great adventure and purpose.

As a fierce growl rumbled ahead in the darkness, she smiled suddenly, and rushed forward with a fierce cry of her own....

ABOUT THE AUTHOR

Marilyn Hudson holds degrees in History and Library Studies from the University of Oklahoma and has spent decades in the research and reference field.

Her knack for uncovering forgotten stories has helped her bring history to life in such nonfiction works as *When Death Rode The Rails* and *Hell's Half Acre, Murderous Marriage, Into Oblivion (2016)* as well as others.

Her chilling collection of short tales, *The Bones of Summer*, her horror suspense novel, *The Mound*, and her history of storytelling in Oklahoma, *Stories Center Stage*, have been well received. She is author of upcoming work, The Adventures of Madame Delaine, featuring a steam punk sleuth. She lives in Norman, Oklahoma.

Historical Note

Ancient deities from Sumerian religion inspired the main characters of this series, Anath, Asherah, Dagon and Hadad. It is thought these are some of the oldest such figures in human history and come from what is thought to be one of the first civilizations. The figure of Anath reflects the confusing goddess who will later merge with the Greek Athena and the Roman Diana. She is on one hand a bloody temptress killer and the other a virgin/Mother figure. Sometimes she is depicted as a sister of Bael (Hadad) and sometimes his consort and at other times a confusing combination of both.

Writers like to start out with "what if" and for me the question was "what if these were based on real people? What if these people over time, and as various successive generations of patriarchal cultures reshaped them, became the conflicted and confusing deities seen today in these ancient records?"

The nucleus of what would become the Anath Cycle was born.

Whorl Books

"Your clue to great reading"

www.whorlbooks.blogspot.com

Barnes & Noble and Amazon

www.ingramcontent.com/pod-product-compliance
Lightning Source LLC
Chambersburg PA
CBHW020726210626
46807CB00016B/319